Enlighten My Senses™

A Path to Open Your Heart and
Illuminate Your Soul's Purpose

By: Cintra Best

Halo ●●●●
Publishing International

Cintra Best teaches from her own personal life experiences, education and does not teach traditional Native American Ceremony.

It's A Jungle Out There
Words and Music by Randy Newman
Copyright (c) 2003 RANDY NEWMAN MUSIC and USA NETWORK PUBLISHING LLC.
All Rights for USA NETWORK PUBLISHING LLC. Administered by UNIVERSAL MUSIC CORP.
All Rights Reserved Used by Permission
Reprinted with Permission of Hal Leonard Corporation

ISBN: 978-1-61244-201-3
Library of Congress Control Number: 2013920398

Printed in the United States of America

 Published by Halo Publishing International
AP# 726
P.O Box 60326
Houston, Texas 77205
Toll Free 1-877-705-9647
Website: www.halopublishing.com
E-mail: contact@halopublishing.com

~Enlighten My Senses~

"Come walk with me and set your heart free"

Enlighten:

to give intellectual or spiritual light to; instruct; impart
knowledge to

My:

the nominative singular pronoun, used by a speaker in
referring to himself or herself.

Senses:

any of the faculties, as sight, hearing, smell, taste,
or touch, by which humans and animals perceive stimuli
originating from outside or inside the body.

to perceive (something) by the senses; become aware of.

to grasp the meaning of; understand

By:

Cintra Best

~Table of Contents~

~Dedication Page~

To Creator God:
Thank you for my life and the spark
of you that is in me; may it help all those
who come into my path and may they
light up their spark of you in them.
I love you.

To my husband Steve:
I am grateful for you and all
the lessons we have learned together.
We transformed our relationship and our hearts.
Thank you, and I love you.

My son Ryan:
You are my sunshine....
May you take the good and the bad
and learn from them both.
Thank you for being my son.
I love you.

~Let There Be LIGHT ~

"While I am in the world, I am the light of the world."
~John 9:5

"We are not here to have beliefs."
"We are here to be the light."
~Swami Maa

"This little light of mine, I'm gonna let it shine."
~Harry Dixon Loes

"Becoming enlightened is finding your own light
and shining it for other people."
~Louise Hay

"In the same way, let your light shine before others,
that they may see your good deeds
and glorify your Father in heaven."
~Matthew 5:16

"We can easily forgive a child who is afraid of the dark; the
real tragedy of life is when men are afraid of the light."
~Plato

"You have to find what sparks a light in you so that you in
your own way can illuminate the world."
~Oprah Winfrey

~Preface~

I am no different from you. I am a human trying the best I can to understand myself, have happiness and get through this thing called life. I had questions about God, humanity and this place called earth. No one could answer my questions so that I felt like I had the answers that were right for me. All was not well in my soul. This book is a piece of the quest that is my life, and always with a desire leading the way with this question:

Why is this happening to me?

The purpose of this book is to show the reader that everything that has happened in his or her life has had a purpose, a divine pattern if you want to call it that, for every person, place or thing you have had in your life has been for you to further your soul's growth for this lifetime.

I am sharing my story with you in hopes that you can see some of the patterns in your own life and work with small stepping stones to be the type of human that I am choosing to be, one that would be able to stand in front of Christ and be proud of who I am as a Child of God, who is not afraid ,shameful or guilty of how I behaved in this lifetime, one who cares about others as well as himself, and about the earth, the animals and how we are treating them and it.

I want my life to be my legacy, in which I may leave this place better than when I came. I love life, and it took me forty years to say that statement, to get to a place in my own heart that was healed enough to say that.

May you be blessed and may your heart and all of your senses feel that this is well within your soul and open yourself up to the Christ Light inside of you.

"Our deepest fear is not that we are inadequate. Our deepest fear is that we are powerful beyond measure. It is our light, not our darkness, that most frightens us. We ask ourselves, "Who am I to be brilliant, gorgeous, talented, and fabulous?" Actually, who are you not to be? You are a child of God. You're playing small doesn't serve the world.

There's nothing enlightened about shrinking so that other people won't feel insecure around you. We are all meant to shine, as children do. We are born to make manifest the glory of God that is within us. It's not just in some of us, it's in everyone. And as we let our own light shine, we unconsciously give other people permission to do the same. As we are liberated from our own fear, our presence automatically liberates others."

~Marianne Williamson

May the words I write resonate in the dark places of your consciousness, may the light come gently and bathe you in its warm glow of love as you put your feet on a path of grace, beauty and joy. Walk softly as you "Enlighten Your Senses."

Love,

Cintra

~Introduction~

The first step in working on healing the heart is to understand that you are in denial. You are denying how you feel and what you are thinking. Your feelings and thinking go hand in hand; this book will help you with seeing the patterns in your story. What they look like and will give some examples to watch. The main question to ask yourself when you are looking inside is "WHY?" Why am I feeling this way? Why am I thinking that?

Why do we deny?

We deny what we think will not be accepted and as my teacher says, "Everything must come to love and understanding." That means everything.

We come to work; we come here to Earth School to work on knowing who we really are.

Who are you?

Your heart is the key. Everything has to come to understanding in the heart, and when it does the duality of life goes away. You understand that there is really no positive and negative in your heart only in your earthly body, the crack that splits your heart in two will become one.

The energy of duality is here on earth. We come to bring to us what it takes for us to be balanced.

Hence polarity.
Love and Fear
Black and White
Yin and Yang
Male and Female
It can all come together to be ONE.

We are all trying to be ONE, within ourselves first and then with each other.

We spend lifetime after lifetime trying to figure that out, and all it really takes is becoming mindful of thoughts, emotions, behaviors, feelings and seeing a pattern emerge.

The following chapters will help the reader on a path, a journey to discover who we really are.

These are steps and stories that were a part of me personally, and as I wrote this I tried to relate it to myself and my story so that you may be able to relate some of it to your own story.

My hope is that everyone who reads these words will get a feeling, call it a longing for more information. There are wonderful teachers out there and so much information. The part that is missing is the way of the heart, the connection of the information to the applying, so my hope here is that you will see how this worked on a real human, what this looks like in real form, really to have "Enlightened My Senses."

"The only way you can realize the self is through the physical.
You need a teacher, you have to experience the SELF
to have the wisdom, you need a mirror,
when the student is ready the teacher appears."

~Swami Maa

It is no coincidence that you are reading this book, and you will see that your whole life has been to lead you to your heart, knowing who you really are.

I am using my life as example of things that have worked for me and things that have happened to me that were extraordinary. I am just a human like you, and if I can do it, so can you.....xoxo

"When you stand and share your story in an
empowering way, your story will heal you and
your story will heal someone else."

~Iyanla Vanzant

~Part One~

~It's A Jungle Out There~
~Monk's Theme~

By Randall S. Newman

It's a jungle out there

Disorder and confusion everywhere

No one seems to care

Well, I do

Hey, who's in charge here?

It's a jungle out there

Poison in the very air we breathe

Do you know what's in the water that you drink?

Well, I do, and it's amazing

People think I'm crazy, 'cause I worry all the time

If you paid attention, you'd be worried, too

You better pay attention

Or this world we love so much might just kill you

I could be wrong now, but I don't think so

It's a jungle out there

~My Mother's Story~

I wanted to give the reader an idea of what life was like for my mother and to where some of your own core beliefs come from. You carry some of your parent's issues, whether you want to or not.

"Judging connects you to what you are judging."

~Swami Maa

The words below are something that <u>my mother</u> had written as speaker at an Al-anon meeting. Some of the key statements here I will **bold** because these things were emotions/feelings/behaviors and beliefs that I feel may have contributed to her illness, but I have no physical proof of that, only my instinct. I did not edit this section because I thought it was important for people to hear the words from her.

My mother was a person who NEVER showed any emotions, that I saw. If she did, the only one was anger. As she grew older, her heart shut off more and more and by the time she died, our relationship was difficult at best.

It took me many years to be grateful, forgive her and appreciate the lessons she taught me.

The purpose of this is to get you to look at another's life as the observer. Catch yourself when you start to judge. There is no blame or shame; it is just a story, just like the story of your life.

This is her story up until my dad died. In the next chapter I will show the ending to her story with my mine. These are her words from her journal:

First Meeting 9/2/1980

Admitted to Raleigh Hills 5/15/1981

My alcoholic husband died 9/26/1982

"When I was asked to give my story, I didn't want to do it, because I am not a public speaker.

I decided that although Al-Anon teaches us we do have choices, but when it comes to sharing, we don't have a choice.

It is our obligation to share our strength and hope in order to grow.

When you get, you want to give it away.

When we provide the willingness, God provides the power.

I was born and raised in Denver, Colorado.

The youngest of three children.

My father worked for the railroad.

I was raised in a non-alcoholic home, I never knew my parents to have drunk.

I came from a high stress family which plays the same role as the alcoholic family.

My father had an alcoholic personality; he was a very controlling person, impatient and even hostile at times.

*In my home a child was to **be seen and not heard.** **You didn't have choices and you were not allowed to express your feelings.***

My grandfather on my father's side was a heavy drinker, and my dad's two brothers were also heavy drinkers, they both died at a young age.

My mother, a perfectionist, was kind and loving, a people pleaser and one who would fix everything. She came from a non-alcoholic background, a preacher's daughter of a family of six children.

I don't recall any of them to drink.

I was raised in a church all my life and I believed in a higher power which I choose to call God; I prayed to him daily.

My sister was two years my senior; **she was very outgoing and did all the talking. She was first at everything. She seemed to have me convinced that she knew all the answers. I allowed her to make my decisions and gladly went along for the ride. She instilled* in me that I couldn't do anything: I always felt inferior to her.**

As a result I was shy, withdrawn, had low self-esteem and no self-worth.

I had developed a relationship dependency which is as difficult to recover from as alcoholism and in those suffering from either disease, recovery can make the difference between life and death.

I became a loner.

I found it hard to communicate with people.

I became a perfectionist, to find it was the only way to get strokes and be recognized.

My brother was seven years older, and we always got along well.

I graduated from high school and went to business school and learned to be a comptometer operator.

I was married at 20 years old to a high school sweetheart and worked for the first seven years. During that time I was fired from four jobs.

*(This represents the belief system of my mother, her perception of her life, with her sister.)

Each time I was told we don't want "perfection" only volume.

By then I no longer had any confidence in myself. I felt I was a total failure.

Being a perfectionist, I could not see the problem. When I was fired from my fourth job, my husband said I would never have to work again. I was sure my problems were solved.

For the next seventeen years I became a homemaker and loved it.

Chuck drove a transport for the local dairy and made a fairly good salary, and I thought he could take care of me forever.

After two years of our marriage, Chuck was drafted in to the United States Army and shipped to Germany for nearly two years.

When he returned, we built a new home and started again.

We went to church every Sunday and everything went smooth.

After ten years of our marriage, a beautiful daughter came into our life.

At the same time we bought in to an Ornamental Concrete business, and Chuck was spending 16-18 hours a day away from home, working full time and a part time job.

I was spending more and more time alone with a baby.

I was confined to the house due to the business phone which was run through our home.

I felt tied down. I baked lots of cookies and breads and then stuffed myself to pass the time.

__I had become a sugar-holic.__

I was depressed and lonely and very impatient due to the sugar intake.

I finally realized I had a problem.

I went to the Dr. and took a glucose tolerance test, which was negative.

I put myself on a strict diet eliminating anything which contained sugar, and in 6 months a whole new world opened up.

Chuck continued to work long hours.

This became our lifestyle for the next ten years; weeks went by when I wouldn't see Chuck except on the weekends or for a short time in the evenings.

Things looked good because the money was really rolling in, but we were drifting farther apart.

I asked Chuck if he could find more time to be with the family; his reply was, "You know I love you, but if I am ever going to make it, I have to do it now."

At times Chuck would fall in the door and looked over-exerted.

Chuck had always been a good provider, very docile and easy going, but he could not stand "Change."

The business was growing, and I had all the material things I wanted. __But none of the physical needs were being met.__

We bought five acres of land thirty five miles outside of Denver, and Chuck decided to build again. This time we subcontracted, doing a lot of work ourselves. We put in long hours and months of our time.

I could see a drastic change in Chuck. I knew there was

a problem, but I could not detect what it was.

I asked him to go and have a physical as he had not had one for years. He had always been in good health and never missed a day's work on his job.

He finally agreed to go. The doctor found him in good health except he had Hepatitis.

I was concerned that it would be passed on to the family.

I got out the medical book and read that hepatitis could be picked up from a paper bag or through drinking alcohol from a dirty glass. In my mind I immediately marked that one off.

I had always had so much trust in Chuck.

I decided he must have high blood pressure that maybe the doctor had overlooked and that was causing the problem.

He loved salt and so I cut down on salt in my cooking.

The problem continued, and I made an appointment for him with my doctor to get a second opinion.

The tests were all ok. I was stumped.

I was determined to find out why things were not right.

So I asked the doctor to set up an appointment with the hospital to have an EEG and an EKG test.

The results were ok.

I then just decided that he had just worn himself out due to building our home.

I coddled him and made him very comfortable.

Until one day I was sitting on the deck outside our country home, when I spotted a skunk out in the scrub oak, I ran in to the house to tell Chuck and he was not there, I ran down stairs to the basement and opened the garage door.

There stood Chuck with a glass in his hand and a surprised look on his face. I felt chills run over my face. He immediately disposed of it in the trash.

I said "Chuck, what are you doing?" He said "Nothing."

I said, "Are you drinking?" and he said, "Yes."

We sat down and talked. He said he had been drinking for the past five years.

For 20 years in our marriage we had no alcohol in our home, nor did we have close ties with friends who drank.

Chuck drank Vodka, so you could never smell it on his breath.

He said he never drank in bars; he drank alone in his truck to and from work.

The shock put me in bed and my whole body went numb.

I was totally naive that alcohol could be the problem.

The next morning Chuck came to me and said "Will you forgive me?" And I said, "You know I will."

He said "I will quit."

I truly believed that he could, and I thought everything was going to be ok.

I cried for two months thinking I must have done something to cause this problem.

One day a friend said why don't you try Al-Anon.

Two months after I learned of Chuck's drinking, I went to my first meeting.

I thought that I would get him sober.

I learned in Al-Anon, I didn't cause the alcoholic to drink, I couldn't control it, and I couldn't cure it.

I was told Al-Anon was a self-help program, it did not get the alcoholic sober.

I was totally unaware that maybe I had contributed to the mess our lives had become.

I kept returning to meetings and quickly chose a sponsor and started working the program, using the tools to make a better me. I bought every book I could find on Alcoholism.

I then realized that I was affected from the disease of Alcoholism.

I knew I was sick and I was ready to get well, I learned who I was and that my life did have value.

Nine months after I got in to Al-Anon, Chuck entered a recovery program.

*He blamed people, places and things and vowed he would never drink again, **he said "No matter what I did I would never get him to drink again."***

He returned home after five weeks in detox, it was nice to have him sober, but I felt I was walking on eggshells, for fear of rocking the boat.

I learned in Al-Anon not to build up my hopes and have expectations. Five weeks after recovery, Chuck started drinking again.

He had been on Antabuse* and became violently ill. By then I was truly convinced that Alcoholism was a disease, because Chuck was very tight with his money and I knew he would not spend that much on recovery and then quickly return to the bottle.

Within the next two years the illness progressed rapidly.

Nine months after Chuck got out of detox he lost his job after 25 years of service with his company.

Nine months went by and he never attempted to find a job.

There was no money, but he talked of going into business for himself.

The bills were being paid, and I don't know how.

Chuck was never physically abusive, but the verbal abuse was tremendous.

*(Antabuse is prescribed to help people who want to quit drinking by causing a negative reaction if the person drinks while they are taking antabuse.)

One day he said if he could find the gun, he would get rid of me if he thought he wouldn't get caught.

I then decided that although I loved him, I, too, had choices and my life was at stake.

Al-Anon taught me to have a plan but not to predict the outcome.

God gives us freedom to make choices.

Since decisions were always hard for me to make, I knew that if I made a decision,

I must act on it.

And there would be no turning back.

I prayed about a move for some time. When God gave me the wisdom, then I knew I must make a choice.

My daughter and I moved from our home to my parents.

I had been working part time for over a year.

Four months later Chuck called and said he was deathly ill. He asked if I would come and get him; he wanted to go to the hospital.

My daughter and I drove out to our country house to get him; he was so weak, he could hardly walk.

His skin was yellow with yellow jaundice, and he again had alcoholic hepatitis.

During the six weeks he was in the hospital, he lost eighty- five pounds and was down to skin and bone.

He had three cardiac arrests and soon died from multiple organ failure.

I have often said if every alcoholic could watch an alcoholic die, he would run for help.

Every alcoholic has three choices: to get well, go insane or die.

Chuck chose the latter two.

Today I have grown through this experience, and I praise God for the peace that he gave me and for the Al-Anon program which has helped me grow in many areas when I would not have otherwise been aware of a person's need for improvement.

Change can mean growth for every aspect of our life.

There will always be a special place in my heart for the alcoholic in my life.

So, you see, the story my mother told shows me that:

~ She had no self–esteem.

~ She had no self-worth.

~ She had addiction issues.

~ Some of her feelings that come across the page are: Anger, Resentment, Shame and Guilt.

~ She was so out of touch with her emotions, she thought what was wrong could be fixed in the physical.

~ Some of her thoughts were: Judgment, Control, Blame, Victim, Inferiority and Powerlessness.

~ She was emotionally abused.

~ Her husband was a mirror for some of the characteristics in herself.

The key that I want you to see is the pattern that what she believed affected all of her life. She ran off of the programing in her mind and could, maybe, see some of the issues but was not aware of how to get past them.

She had a lot of KNOWLEDGE but not WISDOM in some areas.

This is when I talk about how you can run something past your head (knowledge), and it makes sense, but only will the emotion be released with it when it is allowed to come up from the heart (wisdom). The two of them merge to release the belief. You then can reconcile it within your soul and release it with love for the lesson it brought to you. Then you come back to balance; you will quit pulling relationships to you to show you this same lesson over and over. My mother never got this chance in this lifetime.

Sometimes you are not ready; clearly my mother only saw what she had in her awareness at that time.

I also think she had some emotional lineage issues she was dealing with in the blood, on both sides. I think we are pre-disposed to certain character traits from our family. It is up to us with our free will not to continue the lineage with the same misbelief.

~Mom's Death~

I was working at a printing company when I first heard the news that my mom had cancer. Things were very strained between us; but she was to have surgery on her ovaries and the doctor was going in to remove them and give her a hysterectomy; it was an exploratory surgery to try to find out what was wrong with her. The surgery was only supposed to take a few hours, by now it had been over six. I received the call at my job, and it was the doctor calling to tell me the news.

I was in shock as he told me, "Your mother had multiple tumors in her large intestine. They are cancerous; we had to remove half of her colon, and she now has a colonoscopy. She was bleeding so badly internally that we had to close her up, but we did not remove all the cancer. She is in recovery."

I said, "I thought she just went in for a hysterectomy?" As my heart is pounding out of my chest and I can't breathe, he said," We had no idea that this was the problem; I will see you when you head back."

I remember getting off the phone and looking at my friend and being in shock and starting to cry.

I went back to the hospital and waited for my mother to wake up. She had no idea what she was about to wake up to, and I knew this was going to be tough on her. In fact, the doctor wanted to know if I wanted to tell her the news! I said, "No way! I will be there, but you need to tell her." So I watched as they told her that half her colon was gone and that she had cancer. She didn't show one lick of emotion. Even when we took her to hospice at the end, she showed no emotion.

This was the start of months of hell for my mother and me.... Hell for her having to deal with her own death and me having

26

to watch her do it. This altered my life dramatically; this was the trauma that took me from thinking that the world was ok to wondering who was in charge of this crazy place and what was going to happen to **me**?

"Grief is stored in the heart.
You have a hard time caring and having compassion
for your inner child with suppressed grief."

~Swami Maa

She was diagnosed in June, and she died in November. Five months and she was gone, and I was totally unprepared for what her death would do to me emotionally. I took a leave of absence from work and went and stayed with her to take care of her. Thankfully, my best friend took my son for that time.

I will not tell you all she had to endure, because physically, it was not pretty. But I will share with you a few things that put my emotional self lower than it had ever been, with just a few statements. There were a lot of things said, but this will sum up the feelings that I carried and made me "sick."

*Realize that as I say these things, it is for example. I have forgiven my mother totally for her actions. Again this is just to show how emotions can get stuck inside of you and cause all kinds of issues. In parentheses I put some of the emotions and feelings I felt at the time that I could not release.

Two statements that she said to me show how much pain she was in at the time:

I was working two jobs when she got sick. I was a single mom: my son was four, and I was really struggling. I was supposed to go and mow her lawn. I forgot. She called me and said, "You can't even help your dying mother." (shame, guilt, anger, worthlessness, selfishness)

I, of course, yelled at her for what she said and told her how wrong it was. But even by defending myself, she still managed to get inside me. I was hurt, and the little girl inside said, "I will never be good enough; will I?" and "It must be my fault that my mother is dying."

You see, even in defending, there is a part of you that thinks what they are saying is true because you are feeling guilty.

This next statement would ring in my ears for the next ten years:

Two days before she died, I went to see her and could not look at her without bawling my eyes out. I tried to get her to leave a tape for my son, and she wouldn't do it. I was sitting by her bed, and I said, "Mom, I just wanted to say how sorry I am for my part in our relationship being so bad. I love you, and I am sorry." She looked at me and said nothing. I said, "Mom, do you have anything you want to say to me?" She looked me straight in the eye and said, "If I thought I owed you an apology, I would give you one".... She died two days later.

These two statements that she said to me confirmed what I had already thought about myself.

I felt I was worthless, abandoned, nobody loved me, it was everyone else's fault, and I spent the next ten years trying to figure that out.....

Physically, I had panic attacks, anxiety, PTSD, hypoglycemia, heart palpitations, allergies, overweight, addicted to food and couldn't figure out what was wrong with me. I was sure that every day I was dying but so afraid to die, I couldn't live.....

This is my story; I hope it helps with yours.

~Where's God? ~

I knew the moment my mother died. I had woken up from sleeping on the couch in her house, ten minutes before the hospice called to let me know. When my mother died in 1995, I remember coming home from the hospice, going upstairs to her bedroom, pulling out the Bible and trying to find a verse to give me some sort of comfort. I found nothing. No words made any sense to me. "Thee", "Thou" made me feel stupid that I could not understand what so many others seemed to get. I had gone to a Baptist school. Wasn't I supposed to be the "expert" of this? I was taught this; wasn't I?

Why couldn't I get it? Where was the comfort that I was supposed to receive in my time of need? Had God forgotten me? Maybe I had done something not to get comfort. Maybe I was such a piece of crap that I deserved to suffer. In retrospect, my understanding now was that this was not the case. But this was how I felt at that moment: that God had forsaken me, and I was doomed to suffer for the rest of my life. And suffer I did. I put myself (and others) through a hell that cannot be described. The only way I know that I made it was from mercy and grace. I come to you now to help others who are in the deepest depth of darkness, which seems to have no light. I hope my experience can be a candle in your way, to let you know that in the depths of fear, there is always someone to show you the light, even when you cannot see it for yourself.

Since I was not aware of anything else, I started working on myself in the physical realm, not that I even knew that at the time. All I knew was that physically I was sick, feeling terrible most of the time, had anxiety and panic attacks almost on an everyday basis. All my friends thought I had lost my mind (which I had). All of my family was gone except for my son, my husband, and my best friend. My husband spent most of his days away from home, working, and when he did come home it was quite late. He didn't wish to spend a lot of time with me because, you know, I was crazy! He had no idea what to do for me, so he was gone quite a bit. My son, because he was my son, became my safety. In those days I always had to have someone with me. I could not be alone, ever. The minute I was by myself I had a panic attack. It was horrible. Everyone I knew thought I was insane, which did not help my condition at all.

I really put myself at the mercy of other people because I had to go with them. Sometimes I didn't want to go, but I did, just so I wouldn't have to feel that fear and cause a panic attack. I was afraid of being by myself.

I didn't get sick right away after my mother died; it was actually a gradual thing. But I made some of the poorest decisions I have ever made in my life at that time. When I had the realization that God had just put me here to suffer, had left me in my mom's room the day she died, it was a spiral of self-destruction, self-hate and self-loathing after that.

I drank quite heavily and put on a lot of weight, packed on probably fifty pounds in less than six months, and I just went up from there.

By the time I moved in with my future husband, I had really put on a lot of weight. This was when I really started having a break down in the physical. I developed heart palpitations, anxiety, panic attacks, and low blood sugar. I was overweight and addicted to food and in pain all the time.

The first night I moved in with my future husband, it was a real eye opener about what I had done. He had a lot of addiction issues, and I chose not to see it (denial) because I thought that this relationship was what I wanted. And back in those days, I was hell-bent on getting what I wanted at whatever the cost. I cared about no one other than myself. I was beyond selfish and, of course, had no idea I even had a problem and wondered why I was sick/crazy. I was in full blown "EGO' and had no idea that the choices I had made were the cause of most of my problems. The ego believes it needs to be punished.

The night I moved into the house, he had drunk too much and proceeded to tear the house apart. Called his ex-girlfriend who he had just broken up with, confessed his undying love for her, all while I was in the same room. His outburst was more than my fragile nervous system would take, and I ended up sitting on top of the counter, shaking like a leaf. I had rented out my mom's house, and I felt like I had nowhere else to go. I had wanted this, and I got it. Now I had to live with the choice that had been made. It was devastating. I think that was the night I developed PTSD. I was a mess.

The more he acted out, the worse I got. The more risks he took with his life, the more panic- stricken I became. He would go out and not come home all night, not call. As I look back on it now, I see that he had no idea how to handle me; I had completely changed. I had no idea what had happened to him and with him working in town and us living an hour and a half away didn't help. I felt like I was stuck with no one and nothing to help me.

Everyone had left me and I was supposed to be a mom to my son. I couldn't even mother myself, much less him. I tried as best as I could, and I have asked for forgiveness many a time for my lack of mothering skills at that time. I was so scared thinking I was going to die.

I had numerous tests done; nothing came back. I had a heart scan and every heart test done because I was sure there was something wrong with my heart. The problem was it wasn't my **physical** heart that was wounded, it was my **emotional** one, and I had radar that would not stop when it came to finding out what was wrong with it. I went to several doctors; they either put me on tranquilizers (that took me out) or anti-depressants (that put me in the hospital). I was at the ER more times than could be counted. I even had to be flown in a helicopter at one point. I was so sick and scared.

When my son and my boyfriend were both gone, it was a for-sure trip to the ER. I felt so stupid. I felt like I was an idiot. It was the worst self-talk you have ever heard in your life. You wouldn't allow anyone to talk to anyone the way I talked to myself. I had the worst self-esteem on the planet. Everyone just kept telling me to "get over it." Since I had no idea what I was supposed to "get over", this made me feel worse about myself.

A friend of mine made a suggestion after I called crying in a panic. I was always in a panic, always running in my mind. Even when I wasn't running in my body, everything was a rush, a hurry. She suggested I go see a homeopath. I had never heard of one. Didn't have a clue but was willing to try, since I had tried everything else, it was my last resort. I was out of options other than the loony bin and that was looking really good at this point. This was the beginning of my journey into myself, the reading, learning, listening and doing from all different healers and teachers all around the world. Finding out what worked for me and what didn't. I tried every alternative healing modality at that time, acupuncture, reiki, homeopath, herbal, etc.

I read so many authors you couldn't count them all: I would say it's probably in the hundreds. I saw psychiatrists, doctors and took medications. If I didn't have money to pay for anything, I volunteered. I found a way, went to schools that were training their students and was their guinea pig. I just never gave up. The process had all started by looking at everything about me from the beginning of this life, and I went on from there, all the levels that I had been taught and researched, the physical, emotional, mental, spiritual and the first thing I looked at was when I was a child, as you will see in the next chapter.

~Cintra's Childhood~

I am going to put little suggestions of feelings/behaviors for you, the reader, to see in this story. This will help you to see the underlying issues that started from the beginning of my life and were some of the lessons I had to work through.

They will be underlined. Remember, this is how I see my story; someone looking in could see a different one or have a different perception. The point I am trying to make is to look UNDER your story for the real one of your life. Any emotion that is not fully dealt with will keep coming back. Each emotion has its own charge, and until you release that charge, the lessons will keep coming.

I was born in September, and I was adopted to parents by the name of Chuck and Charlene. I did not get to them until October and have absolutely no idea where I was for that month of time after I was born. My childhood, if someone else was looking, was a wonderful one. I had anything a girl could want. My room had Mogli wallpaper; I had every kind of toy and great white antique bedroom furniture. Almost every night, I was scared. I was always thinking someone was coming for me, a monster maybe. I don't really remember, but I remember being scared, so scared that in my mind, my sheet would protect me from whatever was coming. And in 80 degree weather, I about suffocated myself pulling the sheet over my face in the summer. I did not feel safe.

(Abandonment, Fear, Anxiety)

I also had allergies, a ton of them, I was always sick, could not run in the grass because I was allergic to it, couldn't play with animals because I was allergic to them, couldn't go outside because my mom was sure something was going to happen to me. Didn't I know that there were people out there that were not

33

good and would take me and hurt me? Well, no, I didn't; and all I knew was that I wanted to play, and so I did. I'm not one of those people who remembers very much of anything when I was little, but I tend to remember things that had some sort of emotion attached to them. I remember getting allergy shots for years that hurt like hell in my arm until it got so painful they finally stopped giving them to me.

(Fear)

I remember I totally loved Scooby Doo and Wonder Woman; in fact, I had a stuffed dog named Butterscotch that I still have to this day, and he helped to protect me from the monster in my room. I used to play a lot by myself. My mom had this thing about me going over to other people's houses. She would never let me spend the night. I think I was in junior high before that ever happened.

We lived in this great house in a suburb called Bear Valley in Denver, Colorado. I loved that house. My dad had a concrete business called Midwest Ornamental Concrete, so we had a lot of concrete and rocks in our backyard. There was a fountain and a bridge, and I had a sandbox and a swing set. I was always outside, in the backyard. The front yard's not so much(remember, there were bad things outside the house!). So I lived in my own fantasy land and created my own imaginary life in the backyard. I had a turtle and a rabbit and for some reason can't remember what happened to them. I had great Easters and Christmases. My mom decorated to the hilt. I always had a huge Easter basket and lots of toys for Christmas and a doll for every year. Even though I really liked to play with cars, my mom always bought me dolls.

My mom was always cleaning. The carpet had to be vacuumed in a certain direction in order for it to look right. Back then most wives didn't work, and my mom took care of me and made sure I always looked like I had jumped out of a magazine. My hair always seemed to have some kind of a bow in it.

(Perfectionism)

In 1979 my dad and mom decided to build a custom home in Sedalia, Colorado. It was huge to me; it had five acres and was out in the middle of nowhere then; it took forty-five minutes to get into town.

I remember they had a lot of heartache building that house, and we moved there in 1980. It was quite the adventure for me. Again, I was always outside running around the scrub oak making up some sort of adventure in my mind, a mystery that I needed to solve. After all, I was Charlie's Angels Kelly Garrett, and I was so smart and beautiful, I traveled all over the world, if only in my mind. When I would come back to the house, it wasn't so great; my mom was always on me about something. She was a perfectionist, and I was a mess, according to her. She just couldn't get me to listen; didn't I know that she knew best? Didn't I know that she was only looking out for my best interests? I think I hated her from the get-go, I'm sad to say. I think that most children do not appreciate their parents until they are much older; you just think that they are stupid and just trying to prevent you from living life. This is what I thought at that time. She was always criticizing me, and all I did was rebel at everything she said. I am sure I was just a barrel of laughs for her.

(Rebellion, Anger, Frustration)

I forgot to mention where I went to school, my growing up years. It was a Baptist School. I went there from Kindergarten until 5th grade, then one year at public school in Sedalia, Colorado, then back to the private school until I graduated in 1987. My mom drove me into school every day, I had to get up EARLY, and if you know me, you know I am not a morning person. I was a grouch and not very nice to anyone who came in contact with me until about 10am. It only got worse as I got older.

My dad worked all the time. He had to support our grand lifestyle of material things. We had two cars, a truck, a jeep, a tractor and 1931 Chevrolet that my dad had redone. What a great car that was. I used to play dress up in that thing and pretend I was driving. Again I had a very vivid imagination when I was young; I pretended everything. I had no life outside except for school, and all my friends had to come to spend the night at my house because I was not allowed to go to theirs. We went to church every Sunday and out to dinner a lot. In fact, we were always eating because my mom was such a great cook; her best cooking was Christmas and holidays. We had the best parties: I learned at a very small age to put on a great spread, how to **really** show off your stuff.

(Image is everything)

My fears with the sheet went away as I got older, but then I really moved into some scary stuff I had no idea how to handle. If you understand anything about my childhood, it is that no one, I mean **no** one, ever talked about how they were feeling, unless it was anger, and that was only on a rare occasion. My mom always had a smile on her face and her hair and makeup done; she wouldn't have been caught dead without it. It used to drive me crazy that she was so fake according to me, she would put on this show for the world, and I guess I wanted that show for me; she was so nice to everyone. I, on the other hand, was an emotional kid. I had lots of imagination, as most kids do, and she had no idea what to do with me, so she did the only thing she knew how to do: make things perfect, try to control me, ignore anything that didn't feel right and cook.

(Hiding behind the mask of who you really are and hiding your real emotions)

My dad worked for Sinton Dairy for, I think, 25 years in addition to the concrete business. He would get up at 5am to leave for work, and we wouldn't see him until 7 at night. When he would get home, he would fall asleep in a brown La-Z-Boy chair in front of the TV. I loved my Dad and really never saw him too much, but it was great when I did.

I don't remember doing very much with him. I know I used to go down into the basement and garage and watch him work on the cars. I, at one point, thought I wanted to be a mechanic, because I loved to take things apart and put them back together. Because he worked for the dairy company, he would bring home gallons of ice cream. That was my favorite thing: food. We used to eat rice krispies and chocolate ice cream in a bowl almost every night when mom wasn't looking. She would get upset when Dad would bring home so much ice cream.

I learned how to roller skate on our kitchen floor and loved to roller skate with a family friend, Kay. We would always go skating on Sundays and sometimes Wednesday nights. My mom was always with me. She did everything with me outside of the house. We got to go skating right up until I fell for a boy there and wrote about him in my diary that my mom read to my entire family to purposely humiliate and shame me, which was devastating. I really had to force myself to write anything with feeling down after that. I always had a sick feeling that I was going to get into trouble. After that incident that was the end of my going with any friends. I had also broken my left wrist* skating in the summer of 1982, and I never went back to skating every week after that.

(Humiliation, shame)

In my house emotions were not talked about and not dealt with. So when my dad started acting strange, I didn't think anything of it, I just thought he was tired from working so much. But I always had this sick feeling in my stomach whenever he

*Emotional reason for broken bone=Represents movement and ease, rebelling against authority, left side-female. –Louise Hay, You Can Heal Your Life

37

was around. One day my mom took me for a drive to Sedalia and on the way she told me that "Daddy has a drinking problem and cannot stop drinking." I had no idea what that meant; I was 10. My dad had lost his job at Sinton Dairy, and because of his drinking, he had run his delivery truck into a building and took off the whole back side of the building. He was fired on the spot after 25 years of working for this company.

I never remember my mom and dad fighting EVER. They hid it extremely well if they ever did. I just always had that sick feeling in my stomach when they were together. My dad did go to rehab once, but it didn't last. And my mom, one day, told me that we were moving to my grandma's house in the basement, and Daddy was going to stay in the house in Sedalia.

I was very upset with my mom, but I don't know if I ever told her or not at the time. I blamed her for my dad's illness for a long time, and she went to Al-Anon, which at that time I thought was stupid, but I think it really helped her deal with things.

Mom told my dad she was leaving him on May 16th of 1982, his birthday, and my dad started selling things to pay for the mortgage on the house. Mom started working as a house cleaner, and when he sold the 1931 Chevy, he split it with her; allowing us to go on a fourteen day cruise in June 1982, six weeks after having my wrist broken, I got the cast off the day we left.

(Resentment, Bitterness)

When we got back from our trip with my mom's sister and her family, I remember my mom calling the house to talk to my dad, and a woman answered the phone, twice. She said your dad must be cheating on me; a woman keeps answering the phone. I said," no way", let me call. I called, and he answered. I will never know if that was the case or if my mom had just dialed the wrong number. As we went out to the house to load some of our stuff to take to my Grandma's, I will never forget, in the trunk of my dad's car were about 35 empty gallon jugs of vodka that he had drank.

I wanted to throw up. Around this time I really started to hate my mom. She used to swat me, and I was not going to allow that to happen any longer. I would turn on her every time she would touch me and tell her to stop; she used to say I was like a cat, and she didn't know what had gotten into me. She blamed it on the food I ate and that I was moody. She used to swat me with this fly swatter that said STOP in bright red. She denied ever doing that to me as I got older.

(Resentment, Anger and Bitterness)

About August of 1982 my dad got extremely sick and called my mom, and we went to take him to the hospital. He was diagnosed with alcoholic hepatitis. He was in liver failure and was extremely yellow when we picked him up. He had been throwing up and was really sick. I was scared to death. He had lost a lot of weight by this time, and they transferred him to a Veteran's Affairs hospital. He was angry at my mom for putting him in the hospital. His family and my mom had a falling out; I don't even remember what for, but she was so angry at them; I think she thought they were trying to take things from her.

In September of 1982, the doctors thought that Dad would get better; he had started to turn around, then his kidneys began to fail and he got swollen. My mom had tried to talk to him about God, and he wouldn't have anything to do with her. She asked him if he wanted to go to heaven, and he said, "I tried God."

Around September 19th, I got a bird; we called it "Lemon." I think mom thought it would help me. On that day, it was the last day my dad was coherent. I was in the room with him and his brother, I will never forget. He was on a respirator so he couldn't talk, but his eyes spoke volumes. He was crying and trying to talk to me and could not. I grabbed his hand and told him that everything was going to be ok, and I loved him. I will never forget his eyes that day. That was the last time I saw him when he was all there. I did not shed one tear at that time. On September

21st my dad had his first of three heart attacks and never regained consciousness. The doctor said he had brain damage and would be a vegetable if he awoke.

On September 26th, 1982, I awoke at about 2:30 in the morning and had such a horrible feeling. I remember my heart was pounding, and I felt like I couldn't breathe. The phone rang at 3:00, and the doctor told my mom that he had had another heart attack and did we want them to resuscitate him if he had another one? My mom said no, let him go, if he has another one. Five minutes later he called back and said he had another one and he had died. My bird died the same week my dad did. The veterinarian said it looked like it had dropped dead.

(Premonition that something would happen, Anxiety, Fear)

I don't remember what day we buried my dad, but I do remember we didn't have a funeral for him. My mom had him cremated, and we were standing at Fort Logan National Cemetery. She handed me a white box about 8"x 8" and said "Your dad is in there." I remember thinking, "How did they fit my dad in that little box?" That was also the end of his side of the family. My mom never saw them again after the hospital, and they were not invited (to my knowledge) to the cemetery. I was 13 years old.

(Confusion, Resentment, Lack of closure, Shock)

I remember coming back to my grandma's house. Downstairs she had a freezer filled with food; inside was Jiffy blueberry muffin mix in boxes. I remember taking one out and just starting to eat it with a spoon. Little did I realize that this would be the start of me stuffing my emotions with food and would continue to be an issue for me much of my life.

(Denying my emotions and Addiction)

After my dad died, it was an extremely hard time for me being in 7th grade. I was always wearing a sweater that I would not take off. It was my protection, I think. As I got older I learned how to protect myself differently, and I took off the sweater, but anger and defense became my weapon of choice.

I am going to stop here with my childhood; I am just setting up what you need to look at in your own life. Look for memories that **you** remember, and see if there is an emotion attached to them. Everything traces back to your childhood: how you were treated, what you learned, family patterns, etc.

You do not even realize that inside your unhealed little child is running the show!

The next phase of the book will be steps along the way that worked for me, mixed in with things that happened in my life that got me to keep going within, learning my own lessons, and opening up my heart. It is a whole new way of looking at your life and what is going on in it!

~Part Two~

~Dream a little Dream~

Dreams as teachers

"Dreams, visions, impressions, to the entity in the normal sleeping state are the presentations of the experiences necessary for the development, if the entity would apply them in the physical life.
These may be taken as warnings, as advice, as conditions to be met, conditions to be viewed in a way and manner as lessons, as truths, as they are presented in the various ways and manners."

~Edgar Cayce

"A dream symbol is the very best way for your unconscious self to communicate to your conscious self.
The particular image chosen - be it an object, a person, an animal, or whatever - has shades of meaning and personal associations that make it the best communicator of some truth about yourself."

~Mark Thurston

For as far back as I can remember, I would get images, symbols in dreamtime. I really did not see the pattern in them until I was in my 30s. I used to dream about people, places and things. Sometimes I would get things in advance but couldn't pinpoint exactly what I was getting.

Dreams were the first things I started looking at when I was "sick." It seemed the older I got the more in-tune I would get with certain people.

Especially people I had unresolved emotional issues with:

44

My mother, father, friends, and boyfriends.

Sometimes things in dreams come to show you things that you cannot see in the waking world.

They are from your subconscious, not everybody remembers their dreams, but everyone has them. If you keep track of them, they will show you wisdom that you never thought possible.

Dreams are symbolic, and you need to figure out which symbol fits with you. What I mean by that is say, a dog in dreamtime can mean many things. It can be a dog (literal), it can be your best friend (symbol) or along such lines.

I have used many a dream dictionary to help with interperting my dreams, (see recommended reading) but they are only a guide tool to help you look further into yourself for the underlying meaning of your dreams.

Keep a journal and record your dreams. See if there is a pattern. Who keeps coming up? Same person? See if there are some unreasolved feelings with that person and situation.

For a long time I would wake up and remember everything I could about my dream scenario, then I would try to put it together and look at the meaning for me, if it applied to my story.

What are they doing in the dream? How does that apply to me? Is the same senario coming up in your waking life that reminds you of your past? Ask yourself these questions, everytime you dream.

Usually the dreams I remember are the ones I need to look at. If you don't understand what dreamtime is trying to tell you, ask for help. Pray and ask for something to help you with your dreamwork and above all keep trying. This work takes a lot of persistence. It is not easy. Don't give up... remember when the student is ready, the teacher will come.

~Lions and Tigers and Bears "Oh My!"~

Animal helpers

"If you talk to the Animals, they will talk with you. And you will know each other. If you do not talk to them, you will not know them. And what you do not know you will fear."

"What one fears one destroys."

~Chief Dan George

I have always had a love for animals, ever since I was little. I was really not afraid of any of them. I actually tried to seek them out. I was fascinated by them; I wanted to talk to them, and I couldn't understand why they couldn't speak.

I took a lot of comfort in the animal kingdom when I was sick; I was really having difficulty with humans so I turned to our furry friends. They loved me unconditionally, and I really felt that every time I spent time in the forest or at the lake or at the pond by my house. When I was searching for God, animals were the closest thing I could find as proof that maybe there was One.

I started learning everything I could about animal connection, what it meant when you saw them, what they were trying to show you in the physical world. The more I started paying attention, the more the animals came. I figured God created me, so he also created animals, so why wouldn't he use them to help me out?

I had one of my teachers, EJ, take me out on the medicine blanket one day. This was when I really started to understand about God and how God is in everything. This is a sacred time with your teacher and not supposed to be discussed with anyone, it is your medicine. But I feel in order for you to understand about opening up your heart, you have to share things with others to understand more about the lessons each step creates.

* I want to put a word of warning here. This story I am telling was done with a spiritual authority figure who knew what she was doing. Do NOT attempt to do anything of this sort without someone who knows what they are doing.

We didn't go to some fancy park; it was just in back of her house, and we could walk there. I really had no idea what we were doing, but I had a "teachable spirit" so I went with the flow.

My experience with a medicine blanket is that when you sit on one you are only able to speak your truth. We started with a prayer to creator. She had me do some work with the moon cycle earlier on, and we talked about what I had wanted to give up in my life that no longer served me. The moon has four cycles according to this ritual. Maiden moon, to mother, to grandmother, to great grandmother (old hag). The moon is female energy; the sun is male. This was a feminine teaching for me, and I was working on fear at this time. My teacher had taught me how to watch the animals, watch for feathers, listen to the earth for signs and answers that I was seeking. When we were on the blanket she repeated that lesson and added, "Do not be afraid of what comes while we are sitting here. Know that you are safe, and it all comes as teaching for you." This particular night we were asking God about totem animals, and we wanted to know an animal for me.

We lay down on the blanket and waited for the answer, and it came as the howl of coyotes. Many of them. They surrounded our blanket at a distance and were talking to us. My teacher said "You are working with coyote medicine." I was not afraid, amazingly enough. My husband used to say," Cintra, you would walk up to a bear, but you are afraid of what you cannot see."

Coyotes are known as being the trickster, the balance of wisdom and folly and how they both go hand in hand. If you knew me back then, I was so focused on healing that I never really allowed myself to play; everything was always so serious. My thinking was, "I am an adult; I cannot mess around." This was why I had six or so coyotes surrounding my blanket. All work and no play are not good; it causes an imbalance in your life.

So after we thanked the coyotes for coming, it was on to address my fear. My teacher lit a stick of fire, a piece of wood (that I still have, by the way, to remind me of that night), and blew on it until the tip was a glowing ember. I just watched and was quiet, waiting for the next lesson. And then she said "Through God all things are possible." She said," You will eat the stick of fire." I said "Ah no, I will not eat that!" All of my fear came straight up to the top, and I started crying, I was worried about dying. I was worried about hurting myself. I had no medical insurance if this went horribly wrong, and I was screwed. She calmly looked at me and said," With God all things are possible." "Now put the piece of wood into your mouth and let it sit there. Allow it to be inside if you."

I wanted to say that at this point I am scared to death. I see myself reaching up to grab the stick and hold it into my mouth, careful not touching my mouth any part of it, you know, in case I get **burned** by this crazy thing that I am attempting. I put that stick in my mouth and waited and nothing happened! I thought "Did it go out? I don't feel the heat." So I took it out of my mouth and looked at it, and yes, it was still glowing red, I looked at my teacher, she said "Inhale the stick. Know that your fear is an illusion that only you believe in." I stuck the stick into my mouth and inhaled and felt NOTHING, no heat at all. This was actually the first time I had really ever believed that God was there with me. I FELT it. Peace was what I felt, that I was so safe on this blanket and God had let me know the presence was with me, I just had to let God help me. A lot of tears were shed that night. I was so thankful for my teacher and her medicine blanket teachings. I had a dozen or so of them with her, and she started me on the journey inwardly, into my heart, where I was really afraid of going.

In some of the worst fear I felt, as I got more down the road, I would start hearing Bible verses, inside my mind. This was the one I heard that night.

"Be still and know I am God."

Fear makes you run, fear makes you move fast and do things that you wouldn't normally do because you are scared. Next time fear comes, ask it, "What am I afraid of? What is the worst thing that can happen?" And pull your emotion back in. Fear is your emotions running "Amok." Pay attention to what you are feeling.

~Mirror, Mirror~

Reflections of yourself

The Queen: "Mirror, mirror on the wall, who is the fairest of them all?"
The mirror: "You, my queen, are fairest of all."

~Snow White and the Seven Dwarfs

"If you spot it, you got it" my teacher said to me. I said, "What the hell are you talking about????" She said, "What you see in another that you do not like, is what you are denying in yourself." I said, "You are crazier than I thought." But she was right. Gosh, I hate it when that happens.

SO what you are saying is: If I cannot stand the way another person is behaving, I am like that?

Yes, it could be.

For those of you who are reading this, BREATHE, just breathe. Open up and listen.

There are many reasons that people come into your life, I can name a few:

Karma

Lessons

Reflection

Projection

What we are talking about here is reflection; it has to do with the Law of Attraction. Your soul will continually give you lessons to what it thinks that you need to know God. Shine a light in the darkest spot. This includes people, relationships, and situations that most of the times are the most uncomfortable ones

50

in your life. This is about balance. What do you need to have in order to be balanced?

Here's the thing:

If you don't listen, you have to learn.

I know, I know, something that parents have probably said to every child in the world at some point. It is true, the more you deny, the harder the lesson.

I was as stubborn as they come, I think.

I had so many people in front of me showing me what I thought or did, it was not funny but the key to this step is to ask yourself, "What am I seeing that upsets me?"

Pinpoint the feeling or the action of the person you are judging.

Look at that. What is it? Can't get it? Keep trying. It will come. What in me is bringing this lesson to me?

Sometimes you have to enlist your friends for help, oh, and will they ever! Who has a friend who doesn't want to give their opinion on something?

Anybody? Anybody? I didn't think so, most of the time your friends are already telling you what they think before you ask for their help. That is why God made other people in the world.

"Really?" you ask," I thought I just didn't like that person." This is a little trick that the ego uses for justifying judgment. It's really apparent in relationships, especially family and those closest to you. They are your greatest teachers, and sometimes you will hate them because it is painful to have lessons. It is painful to go somewhere we don't want to go. Is it necessary? Yes.

In fact, it is the most humbling experience you will ever have in your life, a down on your knees moment.

The day I realized that I was not any different from my last boyfriends or my husband was a come to the Kleenex moment. I had a problem with food, I knew I did, but it was food, and we all need food, right? Underneath that was an addiction and denial that I even had a problem. I apologized to my husband and I know by now after 8 years we were together, he was like, "Here she goes again," but I did it anyway. I would cry and cry and every realization I had, if I could, I would apologize to that person. And, yes, some may think it is crazy and it made me very vulnerable to them, but I would do it again to everyone. I only had one person who did not respond to my outpouring of my heart, and I must have talked to 15 people from my past to my present and honestly most of them were very understanding and forgave me (or so I hope), because, remember, this is not about the other person, this is about you. Your healing, your responsibility, your actions in your life.

Am I saying I walk a road all the time of being aware? No, I am not. I am human, too; and I make mistakes every day, but the good news is I am quick to see my error and can adjust my life before the suffering starts, which is what the goal is all along, **less suffering and more love**, more compassion, gentleness, love for myself and for others.

I cracked my heart WIDE open with these techniques. It was a slow process. Realizations and awareness sometimes come slowly or fast depending on you. Mine came slowly because I know I thought I had not done anything to deserve the way I had been getting treated. You know, "Victimville."

Everyone loves "Victimville" as we will learn about in the next chapter.

~Victimville~

I AM not a victim

Winifred Sanderson: "Sisters, All Hallows Eve has become a
night of frolic,
where children wear costumes and run amok!"
Sarah: "Amok!" [dances around]
Sarah: "Amok, amok, amok, amok, amok."
[Winifred punches Sarah in the stomach]
Sarah: "Ugh!"
~Hocus Pocus

"You want to be sick." my teacher, EJ, said to me. I looked at her with tears running down my face and nose sniveling. "WHAT"!!!! Are you insane?" She said, "Until you figure out why you are doing this to yourself, you will never get well," and with that she shut the door to her office and let me wallow in my self pity.

That was around the year 2001; six years after my mom died and I had what I thought was a nervous breakdown, three years after I got married to a husband who always left me wondering, "What was I thinking?" And, of course, all my friends agreed. They had a box of tissue waiting for me as I walked through the door.

"People with issues, always carry tissues."
~Iyanla Vanzant

Basically I WAS a mess; my emotions were running "amok." The child inside was hurt and I had no idea how to repair or fix her at that time, and I had no idea what the hell my teacher was even talking about.

Victimhood was the cloak I was wearing for the moment; it was always someone else's fault. Why is he treating me that

53

way? Why can't I lose weight? Why do I feel miserable all the time? Some of the main sentences were, "I just don't understand? Why are we here on this planet? What on earth does God want with me? What is our purpose here, is it always suffering? Why do we need to suffer? What is the point?"

We all know someone like this in our life. It might be you. It was definitely me. This is where people get so stuck. Allowing someone else to be the reason that their life is not going the way it should.

Let me give you a shocker.

The lesson is NEVER about anyone else except you.

"If I can't be special in my daily life,
I will be special in my suffering."

~EJ West

All the people, lessons and things that are happening in your life are to help you grow your own soul.

The important thing is to ask….. Why? Then you will start digging, and sometimes you have to dig deep.

So when you feel this way, try to observe yourself. Why am I reacting this way? Why do I feel this way?

When you start to ask questions and not accept the way things are, you take back your power that you have given over to someone else. This is the **first step on the road to wellness.** You have to become conscious of what you are doing, or someone or something else is running the show. And that is your unhealed child, and you will be running "amok."

"Victims never heal."
~Carolyn Myss

~Me, Me, Me~

Ego-Selfishness

*"The purpose of human life is to transcend identification
with the ego. The ego is the animal nature in man.
Ego is a set of biological drives and impulses that control
attention and use it for survival and narcissistic tendencies.
Narcissism creates and maintains the ego's experience as a
separate identity. Understanding the nature of the ego
and its function helps you avoid becoming polarized
by its perception of good and evil."*

~ Osiris Montenegro

My son and I were having a conversation about Satan one day when he was little. He had come to me and asked about the story, and I relayed to him what I had learned in church and school. He listened to the story; then out of his mouth came this statement. "Well, aren't we like Satan? Don't we all go against God with our behaviors? I don't see how we are different, Mom."

*"Sin: An ontological flaw or spiritual imperfection.
A word, thought, or action that is contrary to the will of God
-an act or offense against God."*

~Urban Dictionary

At that time, I was just starting out on my spiritual journey; and leave it to my son to shock me with his assessment of what I had said, but it started me to thinking, and I started to dig.

Evil is *misused* light. Satan is the great deceiver and the father of lies.

So how is this any different from the lies the ego tells you in

55

your head that you believe?

Adam and Eve ate from the tree of knowledge of good and evil. What if when they ate (metaphor being ingested inside) they had the awareness that there was a good and evil. The ego tells you to determine what is right and wrong. That person is a drug addict, so they must be wrong. If God makes no mistakes, then how is this possible?

This belief that someone is "wrong" is not truth and is of the ego. The ego is out for itself, to make itself about ME. It wants to do things for ME. It will push its way in the world for whatever ME wants. It is selfish, only looking out for the self.

Now, Jesus is all about the fruits of the spirit; and it could be said that Satan is all about the seven deadly sins. One shows the way to eternal life, and the other shows the way to death and destruction. When have you ever listened to your ego's negative thinking and it turned out to be good for you or anyone else involved?

The ego wants to live and the only way it can live is through you. You feed it with your emotions and thoughts. The question to ask would be, "Are these beliefs serving me and humanity or are they hurting me and humanity?" "Why do I want to hurt another?"

Inside of each and every one of us is good and evil. We all know this. The challenge is to become ONE. This means that you do not see anyone better or worse than you; it just is. We are all children of God. EVERY one, even the ones we perceive as evil. The have their own part to play in this journey. They are a lesson for someone's soul growth. There are no mistakes in God's world.

What if I told you that this is where I had such a hard time with the concept of religion? My mother was the first one to trigger this in myself. I used to get so angry with her. She would go to church on Sunday, profess that Jesus was in her heart and turn right around and not adhere to any of the fruits of the spirit. Her actions did not meet her words. I would get so mad. I would say, "If this is how you act with God, I don't want any part of it." To me she was a hypocrite. Do I believe that she was not aware of what she was doing? Yes, I do. I think a lot of people are not aware. Just because you go down in front of the church and ask God to be your savior, does not mean you do not have to do your own work. Your own consciousness and awareness has to be lifted up. This is WHY we are HERE.

"Beware of false prophets, who come to you in sheep's clothing, but inwardly they are ravenous wolves.
You will know them by their fruits. Do men gather grapes from thorn bushes or figs from thistles?
Even so, every good tree bears good fruit, but a bad tree bears bad fruit. A good tree cannot bear bad fruit, nor can a bad tree bear good fruit. Every tree that does not bear good fruit is cut down and thrown into the fire. Therefore by their fruits you will know them".

~ Matthew 7: 15-20

Jesus is ALREADY inside of you. He is in your HEART.

You have to FEEL Jesus.

You will start feeling God as your awareness starts to open up and you see where you have blocked your light, where your ego has run the show. It's not all about you, it's all about EVERYBODY. You have to ask the questions and question your behaviors; you are responsible for your life. God can show you the way, but you have to get on the path. This is where everyone is missing it. Jesus isn't coming to save you: he already has. You have to save yourself. You have to be responsible for your actions, thoughts and behaviors. You have the free will to do this. Choose wisely: choose LOVE.

"As a man thinketh in his heart, so is he."

~ Proverbs 23:7

Everybody has a lesson for their soul, everybody needs love. It is up to you to ask the questions to see why you want to do those seven deadly sins. The key word there is DEAD. You will continue to be walking dead (zombie) unless you look at the emotions/thoughts that have caused you to act out on another. You are responsible for how YOU behave. No one else.

I truly believe that our lives are a spiritual battle every day. Every day we have to be aware of what we are choosing with our free will. It is by choice to let the ego run the show as it always has. We have to separate the two. We have the choice: Jesus has shown the way. He is the master teacher of this world, but you have to apply what the teachings are. You have to work what you have learned. Knowledge does not equal wisdom.

We can know a whole lot of things and really they mean nothing: they are words that have no power unless you give them power.

"Unlike power, which has no opposite, force always
precipitates counterforce, whether the opposing
forces are political, religious, or both.
Truth, however, has no opposite because falsehood
is not the opposite of truth but merely its absence,
just as darkness is not the opposite of light
but merely represents the lack of it."

~ David Hawkins

Power comes from within: force is external. The ego tries to force things to gain power, but true power comes from love and wisdom and cannot be gotten through force.

Next time you do religious practices ask yourself, "Am I

walking my talk?" And if I am not walking my talk, why not? When another looks at me, do they see a hypocrite or a false prophet? Or do they see a child of God? Do I FEEL God in this place? Am I showing others the fruits of the spirit? Am I judging another? If you are judging, you are in ego. The ego always has to be "right." Always fighting for control.

Allow others to be themselves; you do not have to have those around you whose personalities differ from yours. Bless and release them to be on their way. Pray for them, and then pray for yourself to see if there is anything you are denying. God has a purpose for them; you may not understand what that purpose is.

"And we know that in all things God works
for the good of those who love him,
who have been called according to his purpose."

~ Romans 8:28

Remember it's the ego that makes it all about us. God makes it about EVERYONE.

~The "I" behind the Eye~

The Observer, Soul Awareness

I was looking in the mirror, crying my eyes out.....AGAIN.

I was talking to God, "WHY?" I asked, "Why can I not see myself the way that you see me?"

I just want to love myself the way you love me.....

As I snivel and grab the box of Kleenex, lie down on my bed, and pop a movie in on my computer to watch as I go to sleep.

I fell asleep with tears drying on my cheeks.

About a half an hour later I woke up, opened my eyes and freaked out.

I could only see out of one eye, my right eye, only I was seeing BEHIND my eye.

I knew it was my eye because my pupil moved all the time very quickly, adjusting itself.

So I was seeing that this was the "I" behind the eye. There was a sense of calm after that. I knew this was a divine intervention meant to show me something.

I was the observer. This was the first time I had really connected that we are not our body, and had gotten to see it first-hand.

"Our higher self when awakened has the attribute of being a silent witness because it is an abiding conscious presence accompanying all experience."

~Deepak Chopra

I blinked probably five or six times, checking myself, and then it was gone, and was back on-line with both eyes normal.

I was privileged to what is called a miracle. Spirit had shown me that this is how the higher self sees us.

The higher self looks at us as an observer, with no judgments. It is like watching a TV channel with actors on a screen. They are playing a role: this is not who we are. We are children of God. God loves us, because it is **unconditional** love.

Why I couldn't love myself was because I had all these conditions and pressures that I had put on myself.

I AM not the body, I AM Spirit. I AM LOVE.

What is **not** love **causes suffering and creates pain.**

This is us; we come to earth to work out our Karma and grow our soul everything that comes into our life helps with that.

This was when I really started learning how to be an observer of my own life.

This is an extremely difficult step. It requires a lot of patience with yourself. It means you do not react. You wait and see if you need to react or respond or just observe and witness.

When you watch all these spiritual people, have you ever noticed they move slowly and deliberately?

There is a reason for that. They are aware of everything but are reacting to nothing.

When you immediately react, you can cause more Karma.

You have to work on your feelings/emotions because they are causing you to react and act out.

What goes around comes around, as we will learn in the next chapter.

~Karmaland~

Reincarnation

*"The recognition of the law of the cause and effect,
also known as karma, is a fundamental key to understand
how you've created your world, with actions
of your body, speech and mind.
When you truly understand karma, then you realize
you are responsible for everything in your life.
It is incredibly empowering to know that
your future is in your hands."*

~Keanu Reeves

I think by now we have all heard of the word "karma," but what does that mean exactly?

When you pull it up on Google it states:

1. "The sum of a person's actions in this and previous states of existence, viewed as deciding their fate in future existences."

2. "Destiny or fate, following as effect from cause."

Allow yourself to think about this for a moment: what I do in this life, affects me in the next.

I have to say this was the hardest concept for me to grasp, I had a belief like a lot of others that when you die, you don't come back. This in turn makes you be very responsible for your physical actions in this life.

What if I told you that, this law is also about your thoughts and emotions as well?

That puts a whole new spin on it, doesn't it?

In Native American teachings they talk about the medicine

wheel, and I have found no way yet that explains this better.

We as souls come back to work our karma which is created by our thoughts, emotions and deeds in physical life.

In order to move past karma, you have to watch all of these things and atone for your actions and deeds, in this life or in previous lives.

Yes, I said previous.

In the Bible it talks about, "It is appointed a man once to die and then he faces judgment," but we all acknowledge that we have a body and our spirit continues to live on. Master teacher Jesus came back into the same body after he died which showed us this lesson first hand. What if our embodied soul comes back for the lessons from our spirit and to work out our karma, over and over again in a different body until we realize we are one with God? We are children of God, so that means, "We are made in the image and likeness of God" and that we are not separate from any living thing. We are ONE.

My teacher Reverend Sally Perry says, "You die with the strongest thought and emotion and heart center," and when you come back, you work on those beliefs that are keeping you from being self-realized.

You continue to be with the people that you need to work karma out with.

This was huge for me to get, and, man, did it hurt.

"You mean all those lessons and pains from others are karma? Not necessarily. Remember what I said about why things come into your life.

But a lot of them are, and you need to pay attention to circumstances and situations that keep reccurring only with a little different twist. Like your Dad was an alcoholic and your last three boyfriends were alcoholics, and you hate alcohol yourself, but you keep pulling in addicts. You need to pay attention; this is a lesson for you. Somewhere you judged another "right or wrong," and as we know "Judge not lest ye be judged."

Here's how I broke this down to the best of my understanding:

Body-Karma

Soul- Records

Spirit-God

Your embodied soul keeps track of all the lifetimes that you have had in "The Book of Life" or some call it the "Akashic Records."

"Upon time and space is written the thoughts, the deeds, the activities of an entity – as in relationships to its environs, its hereditary influence; as directed – or judgment drawn by or according to what the entity's ideal is.

Hence, as it has been oft called, the record is God's book of remembrance; and each entity, each soul – as the activities of a single day of an entity in the material world – either makes same good or bad or indifferent, depending upon the entity's application of self towards that which is the ideal manner for the use of time, opportunity and the expression of that for which each soul enters a material manifestation.

The interpretation then as drawn here is with the desire and hope that, in opening this for the entity, the experience may be one of helpfulness and hopefulness."

~Edgar Cayce Reading 1650-1

You incarnate to work out those lessons in the body, and we arrive or are born in different areas of the world according to our birthdate for those lessons that form our personality.

You always have the spirit of God in you; the ego mind of your individual expression takes the life form in your physical body.

Got it?

Past lives are real. I have had many visions of them personally. Sometimes your spirit will allow you to see this when you are ready. I can tell you, it explains a lot: emotions and feelings that sometimes you wonder why you are reacting the way you are to certain circumstances. Why you really, really don't like that person, you might have past history with them or they could be a lesson for you.

You move past karma when you are conscious of how your thoughts, behaviors, emotions and actions affect you and others.

Your thoughts create emotions, your emotions create your actions and your actions can create Karma for yourself. Make sure your actions are motivated by spirit not by ego.

Pay attention to what is going on, most of humans just go along with the crowd, never questioning what is going on, "This is just how it is," they say. NO, IT IS NOT.

Ask yourself "Why is this like this in my life?" and hold on for the answer: it will always come.

~He said, She said~

I will not blame: I can accept responsibly for my actions

"We create our reality from the blending of these qualities. If we tend to favor one pole or the other too much, we can create imbalance in ourselves and in our lives.

If we oppress or judge, over-control or misuse, deny or withhold energies from the male or the female, it has a reciprocal effect on the other pole and its expression.

This is because the male and female energies are inherently never separate and deeply interwoven within us."

~Emily Laurel

"The masculine is sovereignty, the crown upon your soul. Femininity is humility and unconditional love, the heart within the breast of your soul and together they make the whole soul essence."

~St.Germain

"The new female and the new male are partners on a journey of spiritual growth. They want to make the journey.

Their love and trust keep them together. Their intuition guides them. They consult with each other.

They are friends. They laugh a lot. They are equals. That is what a spiritual partnership is: a partnership between equals for the purpose of spiritual growth."

~ Gary Zukav,Soul Stories

Relationships in my opinion are the most important part of Earth School. Think about it: everything on earth is intertwined in relationship with one another. In my journey, my relationship with myself has been the hardest one to cultivate and understand. So I brought to myself lessons in relationships, a ton of them.

"Mufasa: Everything you see exists together in a delicate balance. As king, you need to understand that balance and respect all the creatures, from the crawling ant to the leaping antelope.

Simba: But Dad, don't we eat the antelope?

Mufasa: Yes, Simba, but let me explain. When we die, our bodies become the grass, and the antelope eat the grass. And so we are all connected in the great Circle of Life."

~The Lion King

I sometimes wish that I would have had this knowledge when I was younger, but then again all is perfect and now my knowledge and wisdom are allowing me to show others as an example of myself and my challenges. I am humbled at the thought that God chose me for these lessons to help show others. I was not always so humbled; in fact, I was downright angry and resentful.

My earlier relationships outside of myself have not been easy, one might say very difficult but by far my hardest lesson relationship was that with my husband Steve. See, before I knew all these words of wisdom, I had to start somewhere on my road to balancing myself, and I have done that with several males in my life, but the most learning I have done from anyone has been from him.

To onlookers at that time, we were a NIGHTMARE, and by all human standards we should have been divorced. At times I wanted to throw in the towel and say, "Enough." Now as I am down the road and had fifteen years of marriage, I see things differently and can react and act differently, but I only could do that by working on myself. When I worked on myself, things around me changed or left, and my relationships evolved.

You see what you are looking at is a part of **you**. This includes your male side (or female if you are male). They will trigger you over and over again, and that is really what a spiritual partnership is about to grow you up. To grow the unhealed inner child within you that needs to be healed and really, if we are honest, a little parenting guidance that maybe we didn't receive when we were little.

I'm sure you have heard the expression "You marry your Mother/Father." This is why. When you have unhealed issues that are for your own soul's growth, the lessons don't stop just because you move out of the house, they continue as we get older. I really think we are learning about ourselves until we take our last breath in this life.

With that said, let's look at my own unhealed male side. I was angry, guilty, selfish and addicted just to name a few, and as the years passed, my husband and I fought like cats and dogs. I honestly don't know where I had the energy to do it. The biggest challenge in overcoming this is the victim mode.

"Why is he treating me that way?" "What did I do to deserve that?" "I just don't understand?" Why, why, why? I repeated this over and over again; I was stuck for years in, "He said, she said." We can fight and defend until we don't have any more energy left, and then where are you? Defeated or so it feels like, and still have no answers to why it is happening and wake up the next day and do it again (karma).

"There is a fine line between compassion and a victim mentality. Compassion though is a healing force and comes from a place of kindness towards yourself.

Playing the victim is a toxic waste of time that not only repels other people, but also robs the victim of ever knowing true happiness."

~ Bronnie Ware

The lessons will keep coming if you don't get it. You can switch partners, friends or lovers. You will not escape because your heart will keep pulling in what it needs to be healed. When I found this out, I decided to stick it out, not to say that I didn't need a break because we separated over three times in our life together.

Honestly look at your mate. What do you see there? Make a list. Good and bad things. If your list was like mine, it was all bad. I had so much anger for him I had to do the forgiveness exercise at the end of this book for years. He triggered my crap every day! In fact, one of my biggest lessons came when I was preparing to do a ceremony and we had to pray, first for ourselves then for someone else. My teacher, Reverend Sally Perry had me do an exercise called Prayer Ties, which is a Native American teaching.

I think I had to do something like 800 prayer ties, that's a lot of prayers! So in some of the prayers I was to pray for Steve so I started out saying prayers for him, but it just didn't feel right. I tried again, and same thing, I would get a few prayers in and wouldn't have anymore. When you are doing 800 prayers, and you are praying from your heart, you start to feel when it isn't right, when it's fake prayer.

I didn't want that because I knew that when you are working on yourself, your heart should be in it. Since I was working on healing my heart, I emailed my teacher for guidance. She was always so patient with me and after she said to me what she said, I felt the tears come up to flow from all the pain of my relationship.

"Dear Cintra, pray for Creator to help you to see the block within your OWN heart that needs to be released so that you may pray for Steve from your heart."

This is what happens in your relationships, you build blocks in your heart. When you hold onto anger, resentment and unforgiveness, you are blocking your OWN heart. Not the other person, YOU. It's your issue that needs to be worked on.

You really have to do your forgiveness work in order to even get to this level of relationship, where you can look at the lesson from the "observer" and see what it is that you are trying to get. Forgiveness comes first, as long as you are blaming another for your life, problems, etc. You will never get to spiritual partnership within yourself or with anyone else.

Now I come from a place of balance in dealing with issues. Not all the time, mind you, I am still human, learning just like you! But when I have things come up, I step back out of the emotion; I acknowledge that I am feeling this way, I do not deny it. Then I look at the situation that caused the dis-ease. Is it a thought that needs to be changed or an emotion that needs to be felt? And what was the thought before the emotion that I need to see? What does that remind me of? Something in my past? Am I blaming another for how I feel in this moment?

These are all the questions you need to ask yourself. It is up to you to do the work.

"When we're incomplete, we're always searching for somebody to complete us. When, after a few years or a few months of a relationship, we find that we're still unfulfilled, we blame our partners and take up with somebody more promising.

This can go on and on until we admit that while a partner can add sweet dimensions to our lives, we, each of us, are responsible for our own fulfillment.

Nobody else can provide it for us, and to believe otherwise is to delude ourselves dangerously and to program for eventual failure every relationship we enter."

~Tom Robbins

~Black or White~

Duality on Earth

*"Life needs duality. Everywhere you will find it, till the
ultimate arrives. The ultimate, the absolute, or call it God,
transcends duality. But then life disappears.*

*Then you become invisible. Then you have no form, no name;
then you have gone beyond. That is nirvana.*

*These two things have to be understood: life cannot exist
without polar opposites. Life is a dialectical process – between
man and woman, between darkness and light, between
life and death, between good and bad.*

*Life cannot exist without this duality; manifestation is not
possible without duality."*

~Osho

*"The attitude of oneness requires something of us that
has not been popular in New Age circles.
In fact it has been denied by most of them.
And that is the embracing of the dark side of life,
in our own lives most especially.*

*We have wanted to be all light and love but have
overlooked one of the necessary means to attaining
these qualities: embracing the dark.*

*Darkness often implies evil to many of us. Yet, a part of me
knows there is no evil; there is only fear and separation.*

*When fear and separation have been bridged into peacefulness
and unity, then the dark is as beautiful as the light."*

~Brooke Medicine Eagle

This last summer I won a hat.

That hat was black and white; and let me tell you, that hat has taught me lesson after lesson about the duality of earth.

What I mean by lesson is that your soul is constantly trying to give you lessons or growth, always trying to lead you in the direction that will be best for you. Things happen for your highest growth all the time! Pay attention! Don't let yourself get distracted by the material things of the world.

Our Ego is out for "itself," pushing its way through life, not caring about the will of God only the will of man and what "I" think is right. The ego is taking and doing what "I" think I need, all the while not caring about who "I" hurt in the process.

"We live in a world of duality."

- Rev. Sally Perry

Yin and Yang, male and female, we all have heard the analogies.

This means that when we are trying to find our heart, we are looking for balance, inside each and every one of us. If you have a partner, they are a side of you. What you are looking at, is inside of you.

How does that look? This is how I understand it:

Thoughts are electric and emotions are magnetic. "Birds of a feather flock together."

"The heart is a sensory organ and acts as a sophisticated information encoding and processing center that enables it to learn, remember, and make independent functional decisions,"

~ Institute of HeartMath Director of Research Rollin McCraty

When you are trying to balance yourself, you will bring to yourself what you need to see, to heal. The people in your life are teachers, the good, bad and the ugly. You will magnetically pull to you what you need for your highest soul growth.

You are consciously and unconsciously always striving for balance on every level of your existence.

*"Just as inside our electromagnetic fields, the electric thought
and magnetic emotion when aligned and integrated with
awareness or conscious purpose create our desired reality or a
non-desired one when in chaos and blindness, so the way out
of duality consciousness is always a third observer or master
guide from a higher realm, not electric or magnetic, but an
electromagnetic/awareness fully conscious and integrated."*

~Astrid Ma Farias Ma

We all know what it feels like to be out of balance, but few know how it feels to be in balance. Most of us are letting our emotions run the show, and those emotions are "sick."

This is why you are here to connect the mind with the heart.

*"So I prayed, but I had to pray from my heart. All of my
concentration and thoughts went from my head to my heart.
All of my senses - hearing, smell, taste, and feeling
- were connected to my heart."*

~Wallace Black Elk, LAKOTA

~The Queen of Wishful Thinking~

I AM willing to see things as they really are
and accept them in myself

"If you have one wish, wish for everything to be exactly as it is. Then wait patiently for your wish to come true."

~Stephen Russell

"If a man could have half of his wishes, he would double his troubles."

~Benjamin Franklin

There is an old saying that "A person will show you who he is, but you sometimes see who you want to see." People show you who they are; but when desire for what you want gets in the way, you sometimes do not see what is real. Like the saying "Love is blind." I always had a tendency to see people in a flattering light, not really who they were. They may have had some of those qualities that I was wishing for, but I "couldn't see the forest for the trees."

Christopher Booker describes wishful thinking as:

"The fantasy cycle" ... a pattern that recurs in personal lives, in politics, in history – and in storytelling.

When we embark on a course of action which is unconsciously driven by wishful thinking, all may seem to go well for a time, in what may be called the "dream stage."

But because this make-believe can never be reconciled with reality, it leads to a "frustration stage" as things start to go wrong, prompting a more determined effort to keep the fantasy

74

in being. As reality presses in, it leads to a "nightmare stage" as everything goes wrong, culminating in an "explosion into reality," when the fantasy finally falls apart. "

When you are looking so bad to be loved and do not love yourself, you can pull this in.

Think about how many times we have been taught about love through the movies. Don't they make us feel all warm and fuzzy? How many times when you were child did you wish for Prince Charming to come on his white horse to rescue you and take all your troubles away?

I did. I tried to turn my relationships to that, and they were doomed for failure from the start. You cannot have a real relationship if it is based on lies. Including the one with yourself. You are your own Knight in Shining Armor or Queen of the Nile.

When my mother died (as you read earlier), on her death bed, I apologized to her for the way that I treated her, I took my part in the way that our relationship had been. My mother did not. She honestly told me what she felt at that time. She didn't feel that she had done anything to contribute to the mess our relationship had become. It was my entire fault.

Now there was somewhere inside of me that knew that wasn't right, but at first I believed her. Just like you pretend to believe something about yourself or something about someone else.

When you have an illusion about something or someone because you thought that it is what you want, this is a scary place to be and can be very wounding to your heart. It has a shade of victim, but you are doing it to yourself because you want that very something so bad. Desire is motivating you and not God's will for the situation. Desire is a tricky thing. When you are in the flow, things come to you. It gets tricky when you see something you THINK you want, but what you are seeing is wishful thinking. It's not real. This thinking is very deceptive and an ego trick that you really have to watch.

*"Insanity: doing the same thing over and over
again and expecting different results."*

~Albert Einstein

You cannot change another, you can only change yourself.
My mother said what she said. I thought she was the most horrible person in the world. It took me a long time to admit that.
I wanted to see only the good in her, especially after she died.
I didn't want others to talk bad about her. I got stuck in wishful
thinking and wanted things to be different between us because
I wanted her LOVE; but she was who she was, and I had to forgive her and move on. She loved me at the level she knew how to
love. Before she died I had no problem telling her and everyone
else how I felt about her. It changed after she died. I was wishing
for it to be different from what it was. Some people spend their
whole lives wishing things were different about their lives; their
mates and their families. They punish those who have hurt them
because their illusion of grandeur is not fulfilled.

You have to start where you are in order to move, in the now.
Not the past or the future. You can WISH for things to be different, or you can LOOK at how YOU can change your own way of
looking at the situation and take action from a place of balance
not on an emotion, desire, need or revenge.

Let go of that person, place or thing that you are wishing to
be different from what is. Forgive yourself. Forgive them.

"I forgive myself for using you to hurt myself."

~Don Miguel Ruiz

You will spend your whole life and time you have here wishing things were different from how they are. Your time here is
short; don't waste it. Work on what you can change, not what
you can't. You will save yourself a whole lot of heartache and
emotional energy spent where it doesn't need to be. Stop trying

to make them pay. You're only making yourself suffer. The only suffering they are doing is having to defend against you. This might be THEIR lesson. You need to learn YOURS.

The question to ask is, "What is the lesson for me in this situation?" "Am I not seeing this person clearly?" "What do I need to do to heal myself?"

Why are you wishing that your life is different from what it is at this very moment? You are getting exactly what you need. God doesn't make mistakes, and all those people you are wishing were different are the best teachers FOR YOU. Pay attention to the lesson, and everything that you want you will find right inside of you.

In your wishing for something else, you are pulling to you **exactly** what your heart needs to heal.

"You can't always get what you want; but if you try sometimes, well, you might find you get what you need."

~*The Rolling Stones*

~Shiver Me Timbers~

Fear and Anxiety

*"More than 3,000 years ago a man named Job complained to
God about all his troubles*

And the Bible tells us that God answered:

*Do you give the horse his strength or clothe his neck with a
flowing mane? Do you make him leap like a locust, striking
terror with his proud snorting? He paws fiercely, rejoicing in
his strength, and charges into the fray. He laughs at fear,
afraid of nothing; he does not shy away from the sword. The
quiver rattles against his side, along with the flashing spear
and lance. In frenzied excitement he eats up the ground; he
cannot stand still when the trumpet sounds." ~God as quoted
in the Book of Job, Chapter 39 verses 19-24.*

~From the Movie "Secretariat"

*"The wise man in the storm prays to God, not for safety from
danger, but for deliverance from fear."*

~Ralph Waldo Emerson

I had my very first panic attack in a foreign country. I will
never forget it. I was sitting at the table with my husband, and we
were eating dinner, on vacation. All of the sudden I was aware
of my heart. This was unusual for me to pay attention. I mean,
I had really been trying hard not to pay very much attention to
anything after my mother had died. It just hurt too damn much
to be alive.

I said something to my husband about my heart. He laughed
and said, "Why don't you eat something, and maybe it will go

away?" I immediately felt my pulse in my wrist. As I look back on it now, I see that I really thought I was dying. In reality, I really was. It may have not been on the physical level yet, but my heart had a problem, and I felt there was something seriously wrong with it.

This was the beginning of years of hell for me. That night was just the beginning of the massive panic attacks and anxiety that damn near killed me or had me wishing that I was dead. I had two more attacks when I was there: and when I came home, they just got worse. I had no idea what the problem was. All I knew was that I was scared out of my mind.

"Fear is the path to the Dark Side.
Fear leads to anger, anger leads to hate; hate leads to suffering.
I sense much fear in you."

~Yoda to Anakin Skywalker in Star Wars

I was constantly telling my son I loved him because I was afraid I was not going to wake up the next day, and the only thing I wanted him to know was that I loved him so much. I could never tell when this was going to happen so it made me afraid to be by myself. We lived on forty acres out in the country an hour and a half away from town. Nobody was around, and when I was by myself, I had anxiety so bad. I had more trips to the ER than I could count. I went to all kinds of doctors. Nothing was wrong with me. All my tests came back fine. I had them repeatedly check my heart. I was sure that something was wrong with it.

I prayed and prayed and prayed for an answer to my problem. I spent thousands of dollars on doctors and tests, trying to figure out what was wrong. I wouldn't give up. Nothing that the doctors said I believed. Not one word. So the circle continued, and the more I had attacks, the more sad and depressed I became.

I was driving home one night with my husband, and I could feel an attack coming on. My husband by this point was extremely frustrated with me. He didn't understand what was wrong with me and why I couldn't just get over it. I told him to pull over, and I got in the back of the truck. I remember lying there and crying. I whispered a prayer to God. I said, "Dear God, please help me with this or please kill me because I cannot live the rest of my life this way. I am too afraid to commit suicide so please just take me."

I had a friend who worked at an alternative clinic; and she said, "You come in and we are going to run some different tests on you and maybe see what is going on." At this point I was willing to do anything. I had already been seeing a homeopath. The tests came back, and they showed that I had food allergies, hypoglycemia and no progesterone. I was put on an extremely strict diet because I reacted to everything. It was either delayed or immediate. Then I had to eat every two hours because my sugar levels were so bad. A lot of my panic attacks were coming from this.

It took me about two years for me finally to get my body well again. I lost weight and felt a lot better, but I still had the fear that there was something wrong with my heart. So I kept digging. I went to psychiatrists, several of them. I went on several antidepressants and Xanax. One sent me to the ER on the helicopter Flight for Life, and the other made me feel like a zombie because I had to take so much it knocked me out and I couldn't think straight. I said, "There has to be a better way."

I started reading everything I could. In the meantime, I could not let my loved ones out of my sight because if I did, an instant panic attack. So my friends would have to keep their phones with them at all times so that I could get ahold of them. I moved around the block from one of my best friends so that I could feel safe, just to make sure that if anything happened to me, she would be there for me. This went on for years.

Things started changing though. It was a slow process, but

the more I learned about myself, the safer I became with myself. I realized that my fear had taken me over. I was totally in the dark side; and I slowly with each thing that I did, pulled myself back to the light. I just kept digging. I tried everything I read about. Some things worked and some things did not but I tried them all, every alternative modality they had at the time. My homeopath said I was the most determined client he had ever seen.

All I knew was that I could not live my life with all this fear. I didn't always have this level of fear. Why after my mother died, did my fear get worse? I couldn't see it then. It took me years to see it. I had a broken heart, and I thought God had left me. All that was left was fear. Fear of the unknown, fear of dying, fear of illness, you name it; I was afraid of it and the anxiety to go with them all. Not to mention this was when I started to have real psychic abilities. I would dream things that would come true. I could see when people wanted to leave the planet (which scared me more). I remember saying to God, "Really, is this a joke? You are going to give me a gift that I can see when people are DYING? This is not right. I don't want this gift, please take it away. This is what I am AFRAID of, I am AFRAID of dying. What the HELL!"

"What you are afraid of is your greatest gift."

-Unknown

Did I instantly become unafraid? No, it was a process, a path, just as I am showing you here in this book. I read countless books, talked to numerous people. Someone had to know the answers, didn't they? In reality all the help and support you receive is only as good as what you use in your own life. The answers that you are looking for are INSIDE of you. The OUTSIDE can only point you in the direction. You will use any means possible to make yourself aware. In my case it was abandonment as a child, the loss of two parents, the loss of both sides of my family, the loss of my emotional, physical and mental well-being and the worst of them all, the loss of my spiritual self. I had completely fallen out of the Garden of Eden.

My heart was "broken" and I was separated from God on the highest level. I was at the opposite end of the pendulum, but I slowly faced my fears and slowly felt God's love for me again. I had separated myself from God. How many times have you felt like you were separate? When you are feeling the lower emotions, you are away from God, but you still have to process them, understand why they came, be grateful for them and finally release the need in you that created them to come. You have to have love and compassion for your dark side.

My first emotions that I was aware of and had to work through were fear and anxiety. Why am I feeling this? What is it that I am afraid of? Is it the truth? Or is it a lie?

It takes some practice, especially when they have been running the show. You might have some STRONG resistance from your ego. The ego wants to hold onto the victim, and it believes in punishment. Question the feelings; they are leading you to the answers you seek.

Fear makes you want to run. You are missing out on life because fear has run the show. What have you been missing? And aren't you tired of missing out on the life you were meant to have?

~The Grim Reaper~

Fear of loss and death

"Death is a natural part of life. Rejoice for those around you who transform into the Force. Mourn them do not. Miss them do not. Attachment leads to jealousy. The shadow of greed that is. Train yourself to let go of everything you fear to lose."

~Yoda in Star Wars

"The fear of loss is a path to the Dark Side."

~Yoda in Star Wars

"Yes, a Jedi's strength flows from the Force. But beware of the dark side. Anger, fear, aggression; the dark side of the Force are they. Easily they flow, quickly to join you in a fight. If once you start down the dark path, forever will it dominate your destiny, consume you it will, as it did Obi-Wan's apprentice."

~Yoda in Star Wars

I am afraid of sharks. Now this fear that I have may have been helped by the fact that the movie "Jaws" came out when I was little. I have had dream after dream of sharks, hidden, in the murky water. Sometimes I just see the shadow, never the shark itself. It's like it is just looming there, waiting for me.

I don't have trouble with being in the water; although, when I took swimming lessons, I would not go into the deep end because I thought there was a shark in there. My teacher actually brought me back when they drained the pool for the summer to show me that it was impossible for a shark to be in that pool. God bless her.

When my mom died, and probably when my dad did as well I just couldn't get it. WHY, why, why? Why were they gone; and after that, the question was, "What can I do to keep myself from the same fate?"

Since I knew my Dad was an alcoholic, I never drank Vodka. In fact, I actually think I gave myself an allergy to it. Because in my young mind, I thought alcohol was what caused my Dad's death. Whenever I would drink it, I would get really sick. I tried it once when I was a teenager and once when I was in my twenties. Never again.

My mom was a different character, since she died of cancer, and none of the doctors knew how she got it and none of them could find the origin, which was even scarier. She was the model of health, exercised, ate right, all the things they tell you to do to stay healthy. When she died, I internalized this fear of death and loss.

I could not look at it for years. Really, to be honest, even in my awareness, for at least ten years. It was so painful; I could not even allow myself to feel it.

I had just finished some ceremony in 2011, and something called Divine Timing happened.

You know that thing when all the stars align and you know that this was destiny. When something happens to you and you have a feeling you were in the right place at the right time.

The night before, I had a dream about Darth Vader. Now I was not a huge Star Wars fan. I thought the movies were ok but not that great. Anyways, the person that I met that day was a huge Star Wars fan, and I didn't even know it.

This was why I had the dream about him the night before. But more than that, it was a dream for me. I took my own teaching and asked, "What do you want me to see here?" So I sat down and watched the Star Wars movies all over again, including the new ones.

Sometimes when spirit talks to you, it's just a nudge, some feeling; your spirit ears are alert.

When I got to the story of Darth Vader, I cried like a baby. There it was, right in front of me. Fear of loss. I had never even looked at it, and wouldn't have, if I hadn't met this person who talked about Star Wars.

The compassion I felt for Anakin Skywalker was huge. I understood how you could easily go to the emotions of anger and hate because the person that you loved was taken from you. Because that is how it looks with human eyes. Like they were TAKEN.

You don't understand, and it hurts, on every level. It was this feeling I had been running from. It was this feeling that my heart needed to feel before I could move ahead. The lack of control.

Death, how do you understand it? Sometimes you cannot. You cannot see the higher picture of the Divine Will at work in your life.

"Trust in the Lord with all your heart and lean not on your own understanding; in all your ways submit to him, and he will make your paths straight."

~Proverbs 3:5

I could not see at that time that both of my parent's deaths would ignite a desire so strong for justice that it burned in me for years. I wanted to know WHY?

A while ago I had a dream of a vulture. I saw just the wing, and then the vulture got reborn and grew back its body into the wing.

I looked up Vulture (see recommended reading). Here's the part that hit me:

"The vulture was considered a sign of confirmation of a new relationship between the volatile aspects of life and the fixed,

*the psychic energies and the cosmic forces. **It was a promise that the suffering of the immediate was temporary and necessary for the higher purpose was at work, even if not understood at the time.***"*

- Ted Andrews ~Animal Speaks

Things that do not make sense to you are not within your control and are the scariest.

This includes death. The ultimate scary guy, The Grim Reaper.

When I came up with the meditation at the end of the book that I have included for you. I had been working with it for a while and GR showed up. The first time I saw him, it pulled me right out of my meditation. I immediately opened my eyes. I thought "Oh, my God! Am I dying?" "Is this why I am seeing him?"

Then my higher self took over and said, "You have got to look at death; it is the ultimate fear."

"All of the other fears stem from this fear, and this is the ultimate illusion. Once you figure this out, you will have it."

You have to realize, there is no death. I AM not the body.

The tricky thing is, you may know this with all of the teachings and belief systems you have. All of the major religions teach this, but in order for you to get it, it has to be felt on the heart level. You have to FEEL God and know who you are.

Many teachers showed this to us, that we are not the body. One teacher, Jesus, showed it best in the teaching in the Bible. In order for the disciples to get it, he came back in the same body just to prove that it was him. Seeing is believing.

"I am the way, the truth and the life."

-John 14:6

Last year I went back into my meditation. I had seen GR many times, and I just went on with my meditation and really just ignored, he was there until one day when I went in, Jesus was waiting for me at the lake. Standing there just like a normal guy. Jeans and everything. Very unlike the pictures of Jesus we see.

I said, "I am humbled that you are here."He said," I have come to help you to understand death. Take my hand and walk with me." We walked across the sand, and when I looked up, The Grim Reaper was standing there, towering over me with his face hidden. I could feel my physical body reacting to the fear I was feeling in the meditation. Jesus said, "There is no fear." He bent down and picked up some sand putting it into my hand. "Use your breath to blow the hood back." I looked down at my hand, took a deep breath and blew. The Reaper's hood fell off and then his cloak, revealing a skeleton. As I kept blowing, the skeleton disintegrated right before my eyes. "You are not the body, you are a child of God." he spoke.

Jesus smiled and turned around to walk away. As I watched him, my chest felt warm. I looked down, and it looked as though my heart was shining, in all directions. Shooting out were pink and red rays, and inside the heart was the OM symbol.

"What time can take is not real,
what is real can never be taken from you."

~Swami Paramanand Maharaj

~Good Grief~

I AM willing to love

"Only people who are capable of loving strongly can also suffer great sorrow, but this same necessity of loving serves to counteract their grief and heals them."

~Tolstoy

"James, I know you have been searching for me, but there's something you must understand. You and Kat loved me so well when I was alive that I have no unfinished business, please don't let me be yours."

~Amelia Harvey from Casper The Movie

"...love knows not its own depth until the hour of separation."

~Khalil Gibran

"How terrible it is to love something that death can touch."

~Albus Dumbledore (J.K. Rowling)

I was standing in the kitchen looking out the window when I heard her fall behind me. My dog Emma, our brown Labrador Retriever, had fallen and was in the midst of having a full-blown seizure. I couldn't breathe. Her son, Tyger our yellow lab, was trying to go over to her, sniff and help. I panicked, ran to the hallway, trying to figure out what to do to help, hollered up the stairs to Ryan and said, "Ryan, please come quick, there is something wrong with Emma." He came running downstairs, and we went back in the kitchen, and he said, "She is having a seizure, mom."

This was the beginning of the end of her physical life. She had several more seizures that day, and I made an appointment for the next morning to take her to the vet and see what we could do for her. Ryan and I stayed up with her the whole night. Ryan held her while she was having the seizures.

I was frozen, couldn't stop crying. My emotional body had totally taken over my reasoning. Thank God Ryan was there. I couldn't even look at her; it hurt too much to see her like that. I loved that dog, and it was terrible to see her go down that way. I stayed close with Ryan to see if anything was needed.

By the time we drove her the next morning, she had already had four seizures. The vet said that because of her age, there wasn't much he could do. He gave her an ultrasound. She had multiple tumors in her stomach, and he thought this was what was causing the seizures. The dreaded word came out of his mouth, carcinoma. She was full of cancer, just like my mom.

He said we could take her home and wait it out, or we could choose to give her a euthanize shot. I said we needed to take her home because Steve was on his way, and he wanted to see her. I made an appointment for the next morning at 8:00 am, and we would come and put her down.

We took her home, and on the way she had another seizure. The vet had given us some medicine that might help her, and we gave her that, in hopes to slow down the seizures. It didn't work; it just made her loopy and very incoherent.

We got back home around 11:30 am. Ryan had to get ready to go to work, and I was left alone with Emma until Steve got there. She couldn't relax and was up walking around, tripping on things, running into things because of the medicine. I had only given her one dose, so it really hadn't hit her yet.

I called Steve and said, "You need to hurry." That was at 1:00 pm. At 2:30, she had another seizure. I put my hands on her as she had it, to try and let her know I was there. It was heart wrenching to watch. This dog of 13 years was the greatest dog. If you are an animal lover like I am, you understand why it is so painful to see your animal hurt or upset.

They are like family.

Steve got there around 4:00 pm, and since she had just had a seizure, she was up walking around. I put Tyger away in another room and opened the door so that she could go to the front door to see Steve coming up the walk. She had been so incoherent but when she saw him, she wagged her tail and went outside on the porch.

Steve came in and held her. I told him that she wasn't doing very well and I had made an appointment for the next morning to put her down. We were crying. I told him I was glad he got home to see her. Since I had been up all night, he said he would watch her so that I could go lie down and rest for a little while.

I woke up about 6:30 pm. Emma had come into the bedroom walking in circles, and I sat straight up. I came out and asked Steve if she had had another seizure, he said no. A few minutes later she went down in the kitchen again, and I said, "Enough, we are going to take her tonight. I cannot bear to watch her suffer anymore. This is terrible; she does not deserve this."

"Life is pleasant. Death is peaceful.
It's the transition that's troublesome."

~Isaac Asimov

I called the vet and told him we were coming. Emma seemed to have been waiting for Steve to get home because after he was there, she got worse. She was walking crooked on her paws, and I could not allow her to break her legs because of this medicine that she was taking.

We loaded her up in the car and drove to the vet. As we were driving, it was the most beautiful sunset. Rays were coming through the clouds, lots of light, so appropriate for her. I had asked my guides on the way to see who was waiting for her on the other side and could I see. I had a vision of lots of children, and they were so excited! I heard a voice say," She is coming soon," I looked at who said it, and Jesus was standing there with the children, waiting for her arrival in the afterlife.

We got to the vet, and Steve carried her in. She could not walk at this point. I held her face in my hands and looked into her eyes and told her how grateful I was that she was our dog and she had been a warrior. I told her that everything would be ok, that we would miss her terribly and that I loved her very much.

The vet came in and we talked for a minute about what would happen. Steve had a bad experience another time with putting a dog down so he was worried that the same thing would happen. The vet assured him that this was not the case. It would be very quick, painless, and we could trust him to take care of our girl.

Steve held onto her, and I had my hands on her also when she took her last breath with us. It was an honor to be there with her after all of her service to us and our family. It was lightening quick. One minute she was there and the next she was gone, and not one noise of pain came from her.

We stood there for a moment while the vet asked us what we wanted to do with her. I gave him a hug and thanked him for helping Emma to a peaceful death.

"I guess you don't really own a dog, you rent them, and you have to be thankful that you had a long lease."

~Joe Garagiola

Steve and I headed back to the car with tears in our eyes, and I broke down as I went to get in the car. If you know me, I am not a sobbing crier; but this time the tears wracked my body. Steve came around, and we hugged each other for a few minutes. Then we got into the car.

We started driving, and Steve said, "I feel relieved that she is no longer in pain." I said, "I don't. I understand the reason we had to take her and that it was the best thing for her, but I do not feel good." In fact it took me three days to start to feel better.

Everywhere I would look around the house, I would see her. I left her dog bowl with food in it that she hadn't eaten. I didn't move her bed for two days. I didn't want to move anything; it just hurt to look at it.

I woke up on Friday and thought to myself, "Why are you having such a hard time with this? You know it was the right thing to do for her." I realized then that this was not just about Emma; it was about my parent's death as well.

I never honored either one of them or celebrated that they were a part of my life. I had never allowed myself to feel the grief of their passing. With my mom it was the terrible suffering that she had to go through before her passing. With my Dad, there really was no closure without a funeral for him. I had to go right into dealing with things after my mom passed; and although we had a funeral for her, I was too angry at her to admit that I was going to miss her presence in this world.

"Even a happy life cannot be without a measure of darkness and the word 'happy' would lose its meaning if it were not balanced by sadness."

~*Carl Jung*

When we came home to the house after we had taken Emma, the house felt emptier. Her animal soul was gone from the space, and I felt it immediately. She had been by my side for years, being my companion, as well as Tyger but two different souls. Emma gave me different gifts than Tyger. I was going to miss her presence a lot.

I decided to let myself grieve. I actually gave myself permission to stop trying to get back to normal, to move things, to cook, to clean, to go about my routine. When my Dad died, we didn't honor him with a funeral because my mother was too angry at him. I didn't have a chance to grieve, things were just supposed to go back to normal.

When my mom died, I didn't acknowledge that I had just spent four months watching her suffer, get sick and waste away before my eyes. All of us were so angry with her before she died, one of the family members called me and said, "Is she dead yet?" Nobody in the family acknowledged that she was still my mother. MY mom. Nobody acknowledged that even though my dad was an alcoholic and had done this to himself, he was still MY dad; and I needed lots of love to deal with the passing of these two important people in my life. I needed to acknowledge and <u>honor</u> these important people in my life.

With Emma's death, it triggered that wound all over again, the unhealed grief. My beloved dog. Her last love to me was this lesson, a coming around again. There had been no deaths close to me since mom, so I couldn't see the wound was still there, but I could feel that there was something hidden. It took her dying to bring it to the surface to be healed and acknowledged.

I am so grateful for her. I am humbled to have been one of her owners. We were privileged with her whole life here. I decided that I would love myself enough to let myself grieve. I lit candles for my parents and for her. I recounted all the ways she had made my life better. I recounted and was thankful for both of my parents' lives. I HONORED all of them.

You cannot bypass grief; you have to feel it. It has to be acknowledged just like any other emotion, and it will come around again. Trust me, our time here is short. Celebrate the time you have here and with the people and animals you love. Appreciate that you have them, for who knows how fast you or they will be gone. No one is getting out of here alive. Be aware and choose to use your time wisely.

"The soul is the same in all living creatures,
although the body of each is different."

~Hippocrates

~I "second" that emotion~

Emotions and Feelings Open the Heart

Rannulph Junnah: "Now, the question on the table is how drunk is drunk enough? And the answer is that it's all a matter of brain cells."

Hardy Greaves: "Brain cells?"

Rannulph Junnah: "That's right, Hardy. You see every drink of liquor you take kills a thousand brain cells. Now that doesn't much matter 'cos we got billions more. And first the sadness cells die so you smile real big. And then the quiet cells go so you just say everything real loud for no reason at all. That's ok because the stupid cells go next, so everything you say is real smart. And finally, come the memory cells. These are tough sons of bitches to kill."

~The Legend of Baggar Vance

How many times have you heard someone apologize for crying? That is the DUMBEST thing. I realize that if our society was more accepting of emotions and feelings, this would not be the case. When you have a feeling or an emotion, most people deny they are having it. The only emotion humans seem to be comfortable with is anger. The problem is they do not move **past** the anger to see what is underneath. So why is it ok to express anger but none of the other emotions or feelings?

When the mind causes you to have emotions and feelings about something, they are MESSY. People don't want to look at them because we judge ourselves as messed up.

"Emotions are cross cultural – the same all over the world.
Feelings are a subset of all of our mind-body states
(disappointment, hunger, hope, etc. There are hundreds of
them!). Feelings are a learned response in the culture in which
you grow up (the family, the peers, the community, etc.) "

~Eric Jensen Ph.D.

Feeling God is an emotional experience, not a believing experience. If God is about belief, then that is what it is, a belief, like the statement, "I believe in God'" and you may, but when God is in your heart you FEEL it. You can't feel it if you are stuffing all of the other emotions, there is no room for God.

"I'm just going to run into the kitchen and
make a sandwich, there's safety in sandwiches. "

~Russ Duritz (The Kid)

Think of it this way. Emotions are energy. Feelings are energy. They have a current in our bodies. Some emotions have a lot of energy backing them. They may cause outbursts because you have spent so many years not dealing with them. They may cause you to hurt another because you FEEL they have hurt you.

In order for you to start taking away the charge that the emotions that have built up, you must do your forgiveness work.

"Father forgive them for they know not what they do. "

–Luke 23:34

Reverend Sally Perry says "<u>Forgiveness is the key that un-locks the heart</u>." I think you cannot feel God if you have blocks of emotions from this lifetime or previous lifetimes built up inside of you.

"You take your strongest thought and emotion
and heart center with you when you die. "

–Rev. Sally Perry

I decided that I was going to work on all my crap so I could feel God. So I could feel my heart again. At first all I felt was fear and anxiety, but at least I was feeling something instead of being numb (zombie). After that I felt anger and a lot of shades and cousins of feelings. I worked on every one of them that came up.

Over and over again the same process, something came up. I stopped and felt if it needed to be forgiven or if it was a belief or a thought that needed to be changed. I stopped denying that I felt things, even if the feeling I judged was not correct, I still allowed the feeling.

Dr. Alexander: "Why are you so upset?"

Russ Duritz: "Because I am having HALLUCINATIONS and I am asking you to make them go away with powerful medication that I can pick up on my way to work."

~The Kid

It is just like when you FEEL that someone is treating you poorly and in reality they have no idea what you are talking about. You need to work on the feeling. Sometimes that requires you to communicate with the very person who is invoking the feeling. Most people do not have the courage to do this. It takes courage to be willing to LISTEN to another's point of view. Maybe they had no idea what they were doing or maybe they did. You will never know this and be able to process the feelings if you do not step up and ask.

People want to hold onto their hurt feelings, and they think their feelings are protecting themselves. The only thing it is protecting is your arrogance and pride and need to be "right." Your need to be "separate" from them. If they are not responsive to your communication, then you will need to do your own work as best as you can. Sometimes they are not ready to look at themselves. Forgive them and move on. Do not seek them out if this will cause problems for them in their current life and relationships. Try to do the work on your own, and if that does not resolve it, ask spirit for support and let the universe bring it around again, at the right time, to reconcile.

Let me ask you a question. Do we not all have hearts? Do we not all have souls? So how is anyone different from you? It is our personality that is different. Our physical form expressing our God self. So how are you expressing your God self? Is it fear? Is it anger? Resentment? Jealousy? Bitterness? Hopelessness? If it is not the fruits of the spirit, it is not the spirit of God.

"But the fruit of the Spirit is love, joy, peace, forbearance, kindness, goodness, faithfulness, gentleness and self-control."

~Galatians 5: 22-23

Those lower emotions will keep you away from God and away from your heart. Those emotions come from your head, not your heart. They have to be processed out with release. I used a lot of tears for release.

"When we direct our thoughts properly, we can control our emotions..."

~W. Clement Stone

My husband would take me to breakfast in the morning at a restaurant; we would go early, around 7am. Every day we would start talking about things, and every day, I would get triggered by what we were talking about, and I would start to cry in the restaurant. See, when I would wake up, my dreams would give me clues at where I was stuck, so when we went to breakfast, I would say, "I had the weirdest dream last night," and then it was on. I had to be able to see what the pattern was that was causing the feeling, and my dreams would help me to do that.

In the morning before you eat, your vibration is higher than normal from sleeping. I say it is like fasting. Eating some foods lowers your vibration, and fasting can make it higher. Then you are able to receive things from spirit. The word "break-fast" "literally means to break the fasting period of the prior night."

I became really familiar with all the waitresses in the restaurant, and after I explained that I was ok and my husband was not upsetting me, they would bring me a box of Kleenex and leave it on the table for me. This went on for at least a year. I was extremely hurt and had a lot of healing to do in my heart. A lot of damage had been done because of my life story, and a lot of damage had been done caused by me.

I believe there are several types of crying. One is a victim cry. We have all heard someone. It sounds like this, "I cannot believe that they did that to me" or "I do not deserve the way they have been treating me." This cry comes from your perceiving that someone outside of you is the cause of all your trouble. It usually has anger behind it and hurt underneath it.

"The heart is connected to spirit, if your heart is not connected to spirit, the heart will deliver messages to the body so that you will look at the issue."

~EJ West

Then there is a trigger cry, like what I reference above. When you have someone say something to you, you see something on the outside that resonates somewhere inside with a belief, and causes you to react. For example, when someone says, "Oh honey, you are so beautiful, you should be proud of yourself." You might have a belief that you are not, so this can make tears come to your eyes. You do not believe what they are saying. This causes a conflict in the mind/body/spirit. You hear the statement, going through your mind which has a belief that is running like, "I am ugly, and I can't do anything." Your spirit heart knows this is not true, so there is a separation, and this makes you cry. Your heart and head are not aligned. You need to step back without judgment of yourself (observer) and look at what just happened (the observed).

"Everything that passes through the filter of your mind has to go through the belief system to get to you."

~ EJ West

Why are you crying?

One of my biggest lessons in my life came from that question. I was at a retreat volunteering. I would do whatever I had to do just to be around spiritual people, to learn from them. This weekend a Swami from India was in Colorado, and we were up in Bailey at a house for a weekend retreat.

When I came into a room with all these healers, I could do nothing but cry. I could not understand it. In fact, whenever I would try to talk to any of these people I would cry, and I could not speak. I sometimes had to write down my question just to get it answered.

This day, Swami Paramanand Ji Maharaj, came over to me with his translator and spoke to me. He looked at me and said, "Why are you crying?" I told him, "I don't know." He said to me, "Come back and tell me when you know." It took me at least a day to figure it out what I was feeling and why it was causing me to cry. So when I had the answer, I went over to talk to him again. I said, "I know why I am crying. I feel that I am unworthy to be in your presence" and started crying again.

He smiled and came over and took my hand (which is an honor I found out later). He spoke so gently to me. He said, "Good, realize I am no better than you, I just know who I am, and you are learning who you are. You are on the path to self-realization." With that he let go of my hand and walked away.

I have never forgotten it. In that moment my whole brain rewired, or so it seemed.

The third cry is the soul cry. This cry comes when you have reconciliation in the heart. This cry is the game changer, and

you will FEEL the change in your body. I call it the domino effect. It's like you start with one belief, and all the other beliefs
that have come after the one on your tree of knowledge tumble
down, and you get it all the way to the root. Soul cry comes
when the grace of God is with you. In my experience it can come
in ceremony, church, meditation or with a spiritual authority figure. This is how it came to me. It will set you free when you
realize the lie that you believed (in your head) comes down to
the emotional heart and releases. It's a life changer.

*"Every experience we have reveals to us a word in the
language of our own wisdom."*

~ Mark Nepo

Your beliefs, feelings and emotions are the key to your heart,
"forgiveness unlocks the heart," and crying is the washing energy of the heart. All of these together open it wide. Sometimes I
felt I couldn't cry anymore. Slowly I started not to cry as much,
after I questioned the beliefs and quit believing the lies that others had told me and I told myself. I had PEACE. For the first time
in my life, I had moments of peace and balance; they started to
get more and more. Now when I have an emotion, they do not
come up as often, if it does, I look at what is causing it. A belief?
A lie? A bad day? What is going on? This is the way of the heart.

I can say it is like the "Wizard of Oz." You need knowledge,
courage and heart. The knowledge has to be turned into wisdom;
knowledge alone is just "knowing" not "getting." Courage is
needed for the days and nights of suffering, lack of understanding and the question, "Why is this happening to me?" This work
is not for the weak or victim. Heart is the most important of them
all; everything that you desire is inside of you.

"If I ever go looking for my heart's desire again, I won't look any further than my own back yard. Because if it isn't there, I never really lost it to begin with."

~ L. Frank Baum, the Wonderful Wizard of Oz

"Nor will they say, 'See here!' or 'See there!' For indeed, the kingdom of God is within you."

~ Luke 17:21

~A Pot to Thonder~

Perception, a thought to ponder

"A human being is a part of the whole called by us universe, a part limited in time and space. He experiences himself, his thoughts and feeling as something separated from the rest, a kind of optical delusion of his consciousness. This delusion is a kind of prison for us, restricting us to our personal desires and to affection for a few persons nearest to us. Our task must be to free ourselves from this prison by widening our circle of compassion to embrace all living creatures and the whole of nature in its beauty."

~Albert Einstein

I just finished seeing, "OZ, the great and powerful." When I walked out of the theater, my mind was running, as it usually does, since I am always working to see the bigger picture. Looking beneath things, to see the lessons underneath what is going on.

I came home, and my son and I were talking about the movie and how it fit into the first part of the "Wizard of Oz." I said to him, "Here's a pot to thunder." He looked at me and laughed and said, "Mom, you said it wrong." So I tried to say it again, and it came out the same way. A pot to thonder.

I said, "This movie, to me, is all about perception."

Perception is a tricky thing, since your perceptions of situations are tainted because of your beliefs and judgments about the thing you are looking at. When you see something that you think is evil or bad, there is a belief system running through your mind. The thing that you don't see is what is happening behind the scenes in this person's life. This person might need to have this lesson, and humanity as a whole might need to have this lesson, but you only see that this lesson is painful and has hurt you, so you deem it as "bad or evil."

For example, in the movie there are sisters, one sister in particular I am going to talk about, Theodora. In the movie she starts out having a crush on Oz, the master manipulator. He does not think about how his lies and deceit have affected her or are going to affect her (karma); he is only concerned with himself (ego) and what he is going to receive being king of Oz.

As the story progresses, and her jealous sister, Evanora, gets involved, (she also is only out for herself, her ego) decides to tell her sister gossip, and Theodora gets her heart broken. We all know what happens when your heart gets broken. You are never going to let that EVER happen again. In the movie she takes this to a whole new level. She shuts off her heart totally; we get to see the wicked witch who is so evil in the "Wizard of Oz" from long ago. She tries to wreak havoc with vengeance on the Oz people and Oz himself; but, of course, in the end she flies off on her broom, and this sets it up for the original movie from 1939.

So this is like a pre-story to the first movie. We get to see the beginning of the story.

What if I said, this is how life is? You really have no idea what is going on behind the scenes and in people's lives. One of the many reasons for people's suffering is this one lesson. You are judging that this is not the way it should be because it hurt you personally or hurt someone else close to you, but what you are not looking at is the bigger picture.

So as you are watching the movie, you find yourself having compassion and understanding for Theodora; at least I did. It provides you understanding as to why she acts the way she does, and you can find it in your heart to forgive her in a sense because you know her STORY. It sets the story up for the first movie and why she is so evil and we, the audience in watching the first movie, think she is just evil and wants to do others harm for no reason. We hate that witch, how she scares the characters, how she manipulates and seeks revenge. Without the villain, we would not have the heroine. Nothing inspires people more than if they think that good wins over evil, right?

Jesus said, "Father, forgive them, for they do not know what they are doing."

~Luke 23:34

It is just like this in life, since you do not always get to see the bigger picture in your own life or in another's. It can look on the outside that it is unfair, unjust. Who is running this show anyway?

"And we know that in all things God works for the good of those who love him, who have been called according to his purpose."

~Romans 8:28

Our perception is not DIVINE perception, but we may get a glance at what is going on to have more understanding for ourselves. My higher self has shown me this many times but sometimes you don't understand, or you are not ready to see the whole picture. We can pray for clarity to help our own soul's growth and why it came to be in our life. Then we can release it letting go of trying to **know**; it is not within our power to understand at this time.

"Trust in the Lord with all your heart and lean not on your own understanding."

~ Proverbs 3:5

Letting things be exactly the way they are with no judgment, you can understand the witch and her acting out her pain on others because she is hurt, in her heart. Does this condone her behavior? No. Am I saying that you should overlook her acts? No. This way of thinking helps YOU to reconcile "why" this is happening. It is about you, your soul. Not the selfishness of the ego about you, the soul lesson about us.

The karma that she is accruing is about her, but your reaction and how you put yourself in HER story is yours. So you move out of good vs. evil and become the observer, which is just a change in perception. A new thought to ponder.

"Change the way you look at things,
and the things you look at change."

- Wayne W. Dyer

~I've got the Power~

I will use my power for good

"Tat Tvam Asi- I see the other in myself and myself in others."

~Deepak Chopra

"With great power there must also come ... great responsibility!"

~STAN LEE, Amazing Fantasy #15, Aug. 1962

"Perhaps those who are best suited to power are those who have never sought it. Those who ... have leadership thrust upon them, and take up the mantle because they must, and find to their own surprise that they wear it well."

~J. K. ROWLING, Harry Potter and the Deathly Hallows

"He who controls others may be powerful, but he who has mastered himself is mightier still."

~Tao Te Ching

One of the things that still triggers me to this day is the power and control dynamic within relationships. There is an interplay all the time with people on different levels of this. When we act to have power and control over another, we are choosing to make another do what we think they need to do.

It could be that you perceive someone does you a wrong, and in retaliation, we extend our power over the situation. We force and manipulate the circumstance because it can prevent things from happening to us and bends the situation to our will. You see, it is always about the person trying to extend the control over another.

*"Nearly all men can stand adversity, but if you want to
test a man's character, give him power."*

~Abraham Lincoln

They are afraid; it is fear underneath the power trip. There
are so many reasons that this dynamic can get triggered; and
when it is activated, it is a trust killer. When someone uses their
power and control on you, you lose your trust in them. You lose
your respect, and there is always this little voice in the back of
your mind that says, "Will they do it again?" It can start to chip
away at the house you have built together; and if it keeps happening, the house will crumble.

No one is better than anyone else. No one has the right to
bully and try to control you. Some of us have made choices
in our lives that have had consequences. You do something to
break the law; you will have a day of reckoning. When you misuse your power, you will also have a day of reckoning. Will it
be in this life, I do not know; but I know that what goes around
comes around.

Relationships make you vulnerable. The person who you
are with knows your deepest darkest secrets. They know how to
upset you, and they know how to love you. Respect the person
you are with or have an interaction with. They are human beings. You can act with honor and integrity in the worst of circumstances. Do not use their vulnerability against them, because
someday that person might be you.

*"The bigger they are, the harder they fall. And the better the
world liked seeing them fall."*

~Loretta Chase, Lord of Scoundrels

Some of us are more fortunate than others; we do not need
to say that we are better because of this. This makes and breeds

jealousy and envy. Use your power for good, not darkness. If you are a boss, you would not be where you are without the employees in your company beneath you. Respect your workers and anyone in service to you. If you are a leader, it is your responsibility to be a great leader, God chose you for this position, and you can lose your power just as fast. Nobody wants to do anything for a jerk. Some of the best bosses I know are the ones who dig in and work right alongside their workers.

When someone else is picking up after you, even if you are paying them, have respect for them. Just because you are staying in a hotel that isn't yours, pick up after yourself. Make someone's job easier; leave them an anonymous note of thanks.

Random acts of kindness are a good way to exert control, over YOU. You get to control the gift and how to give it. If you are buying something for someone, do not expect anything in return, that again is a shade of control. "If I buy so and so this, then they will owe me," and then you get to pull out your gift and use it as a weapon against someone later.

Respect your partner. You would not be where you are without that person. It takes two in a relationship. Honor that dynamic, do not abuse your power just because you can.

"So I had to be careful. I recognized the responsibility that,
whether I liked it or not,
I had to accept whatever the obligation was.
That was to behave in a manner, to carry myself in such a
professional way, as if there ever is a reflection,
it's a positive one."

~Sidney Poitier

~Spiritual Alchemy~

I can transform my whole life with gratitude

"At times our own light goes out and is rekindled by a spark from another person. Each of us has cause to think with deep gratitude of those who have lighted the flame within us."
~Albert Schweitzer

"When you practice gratefulness there is a sense of respect for others."

~The Dalai Lama

"Can you see the holiness in those things you take for granted–a paved road or a washing machine? If you concentrate on finding what is good in every situation, you will discover that your life will suddenly be filled with gratitude, a feeling that nurtures the soul."

~Rabbi Harold Kushner

"Gratitude is riches. Complaint is poverty."

~Doris Day

"Let us rise up and be thankful, for if we didn't learn a lot today, at least we learned a little, and if we didn't learn a little, at least we didn't get sick, and if we got sick, at least we didn't die; so, let us all be thankful."

~Buddha

How many times in your life have you complained or heard someone else complain? "Why is this happening to me?" "Why is he/she doing that to me?" "Why am I sick?" "Why does so and so act that way; that is ridiculous, stupid, etc.!'"

One of the last steps I have learned to apply is gratitude. In order to be in gratitude, you can't be complaining or a victim because it just doesn't work. If I am grateful for the person who is causing me pain, I cannot be a victim. If I stop complaining about another, I can learn to be grateful for that person that they have come into my life. I can accept that this is the way things are to be right now and stay in the present because nothing happens in the past. The only changes you can make are in the now.

So I can be angry about how someone treated me in the past; but if I pull that event to the present, then what is there to be angry about? It's over. If you can't let it go, then something else is triggering you, and you need to dig until you can figure out why you cannot be grateful for the lesson. If I am not grateful for the lesson or the person, then sometimes they come back around again in a different form for the same lesson until you get it, kind of like karma, around and around.

"Second verse same as the first."

~Murray and Weston

Complaining changes nothing, gratitude changes everything. You do not have to be overjoyed at your situation in your life, but you do not have to complain either. What is going on right now is for your best growth. Where you are right now is for your best growth. Every person, place and thing right now in your life is for your best growth, and those lessons and people are supposed to be there to show you about yourself. Remember, "If you spot it, you got it."

Try to find one thing to be grateful for every day. When you find yourself complaining that everything is bad, start looking for what is good. If you cannot do this, you might be addicted to the drama of complaining. The lesson of gratitude will show you this in yourself if you are. When you are addicted to drama, you do not have to look at yourself.

*"If I can't be special in my daily life I will
be special in my suffering."*

~EJ West

The question to ask is, "Why am I not grateful for everything and everyone in my life?"

When you choose to be grateful this will bring in the Law of ONE which is LOVE. Love for yourself and love for another.

"If anyone says, "I love God," and hates his brother, he is a liar; for he who does not love his brother whom he has seen cannot love God whom he has not seen."

~1 John 4:20

In order to transition out of a situation or belief, you have to be in teachable mode, starting with gratitude and humbleness. If you are not teachable, you might think you know it all, and then we do not listen. You might think to yourself, "I know what is best for me." "I do not need anyone to tell me anything; I already KNOW it all." We think we do not need to change because we are legends in our own minds right?

"Pride goes before destruction, a haughty spirit before a fall."

~Proverbs 16:18

One has to be aware of the issues within oneself, work on shifting the energy and being grateful for the lessons and everything else in life. If you can't find anything else to be grateful for, be thankful that you are breathing and with each day you wake up you have a chance to make a change.

When you "get" all of this on a heart level, you have transformed the energy within yourself. When you do this, you affect the whole earth, starting with yourself. Just because you chose to look at something and say, "Why is this that way in my life?" You can be grateful for your life and the lessons you have received. To be thankful God chose you for the carrying out of the gift of your life.

Seeking, learning and applying are the way to the heart.

"If I speak in the tongues of men or of angels, but do not have love, I am only a resounding gong or a clanging cymbal. If I have the gift of prophecy and can fathom all mysteries and all knowledge, and if I have a faith that can move mountains, but do not have love, I am nothing. If I give all I possess to the poor and give over my body to hardship that I may boast, but do not have love, I gain nothing.

Love is patient, love is kind. It does not envy, it does not boast, it is not proud. It does not dishonor others, it is not self-seeking, it is not easily angered, it keeps no record of wrongs. Love does not delight in evil but rejoices with the truth. It always protects, always trusts, always hopes, and always perseveres.

Love never fails. But where there are prophecies, they will cease; where there are tongues, they will be stilled; where there is knowledge, it will pass away. For we know in part and we prophesy in part, but when completeness comes, what is in part disappears. When I was a child, I talked like a child; I thought like a child, I reasoned like a child.

When I became a man, I put the ways of childhood behind me. For now we see only a reflection as in a mirror; then we shall see face to face. Now I know in part; then I shall know fully, even as I am fully known.

And now these three remain: faith, hope and love. But the greatest of these is love."

~*I Corinthians 13*

Following these steps that I have walked will hopefully help you on your path to open your heart as they have helped open mine. This is my wish for you. You will transform your whole life; and when you change for the better, your life will be the light to show others. Not by your KNOWLEDGE, but by your SELF-HEALING-LOVE-HEART-LIGHT, by your very presence here on earth. I hope this book supports you on your journey, and if you received something out of it, please give it to another. Pay it forward, and share the love.

I am grateful for you......xoxo

> *"Everybody thinks of changing humanity,*
> *but nobody thinks of changing himself."*
>
> ~*Leo Tolstoy*

~Part Three~

Enlighten My Senses™

~We are the Light~

"We have to believe we are magic, nothing can stand in our way." ~John Farrar

"The world is full of magic things, patiently waiting for our senses to grow sharper."

~W.B. Yeats

"I do believe in an everyday sort of magic -- the inexplicable connectedness we sometimes experience with places, people, works of art and the like; the eerie appropriateness of moments of synchronicity; the whispered voice, the hidden presence, when we think we're alone."

~Charles de Lint

"Somehow I can't believe there are any heights that can't be scaled by a man who knows the secret of making dreams come true. This special secret, it seems to me, can be summarized in four C's. They are Curiosity, Confidence, Courage, and Constancy and the greatest of these is Confidence. When you believe a thing, believe it all the way, implicitly and unquestionably."

~Walt Disney

"Magic is believing in yourself, if you can do that, you can make anything happen."

~ Johann Wolfgang von Goethe

"Magical places are always beautiful and deserve to be contemplated ... Always stay on the bridge between the invisible and the visible."

~Paulo Coelho

"We do not need magic to change the world; we carry all the power we need inside ourselves already: we have the power to imagine better."

~ J.K. Rowling

"Is there magic in this world? Certainly! But it is not the kind of magic written about in fantasy stories. It is the kind of magic that comes from ideas and the hard work it often takes to make them real."

~Robert Fanney

~Meditation for connecting you with your emotional body~

A prayer before starting:

Creator God, please, walk with me now toward the path to my heart. Guide me gently as I look at things that I did not wish to see before. I am willing to open my heart and heal the wounds from this lifetime and previous lifetimes if it is time. Please show me what emotions and feelings are keeping my heart stuck so that I may work through them with love and compassion for myself and others.

Amen

Close your eyes and focus on your breath. Slowly inhale and exhale, inhale and exhale, inhale and exhale.

Picture in your mind the mountains, and as you walk around a corner there is a lake, surrounded by beautiful trees, evergreens. At the corner over to the left is a waterfall off into the distance. You look up at the sky, and it is blue, with a few clouds. You see a bald eagle flying overhead to bring in the energy of awareness to help you.

As you pull your vision downward, you see in the center of the lake, an island. It has a deer on it, a female, a doe. She is watching you to bring unconditional love to your heart. She is surrounded by wildflowers that are highlighted by a ray of sunshine. She watches you patiently.

You pull your vision to where you are standing barefoot, on the outskirts of the lake. The ground feels cool, and the temperature of the day is warm and not uncomfortable. You inhale the fragrance of the mountain air, the smell of the fresh water of the lake.

You notice the lake gently running up to your feet trying to pull you into it. You walk over to the edge of the lake, taking a slow inhale and exhale again. You hear the waterfall over to your left.

You put your feet into the water, just up to your ankles; the water feels cool, not cold, and grounds you into your body.

Everything is perfect at this moment. You feel safe, loved and adored by the Universe.

As you stand in the water, you look down at the lake, and it is still. You see the dark blue water, and you close your eyes and look within.

You ask your guides to show you, "What do I need to know at this time?" "Show me what I need to see."

(People, places, and things may come into your mind at this time. Try to allow all of these things to come. Keep breathing, and if emotions come up, allow them to be expressed. The important thing at this time is awareness. Be very aware of what you are seeing.)

After a few minutes, all the things that have come to help you start to fade, and it is just you looking at the dark blue water, and you feel the coolness on your feet again. You take a deep breath, slowly inhale and exhale, inhale and exhale, inhale and exhale. You hear the eagle rustle his feathers above and the doe moving in the grass. You hear the waterfall off into the distance, and then you open your eyes slowly. You see your feet in the water. You still feel safe and grounded and step back out of the water. Looking around, you see yourself walking around the mountain, with the swaying trees, away from the lake as you offer this prayer:

Thank you, Creator God, for showing me what I need to see at this time.

Please help me to release the blocks in my heart with ease and with grace. Amen.

You may do this meditation one time a week. Once a week will help you to process what you see in the water or around you at the lake.

Once you start to look within, the healing has begun. Be gentle with yourself; treat yourself as you would treat a small child, with patience, love and understanding.......xoxo

~Words of Wisdom from Others~

There have been so many teachers who have helped on this path to awareness, I always say find one who is calling to you, find one who makes you dig deep. They might really anger you, and if so, they might be the one for you. One who thinks they know it all does not have a teachable spirit and, to be honest, if you think you know it all, I'm afraid of you!

"A proud man is always looking down on things and people; and, of course, as long as you are looking down, you cannot see something that is above you."

~ C.S. Lewis

I have read so many books, I cannot count all of them but know it is in the hundreds. Listened to speakers and done workshops. For a while, that was all I did. I had an acceptance in me that would draw me closer to myself and to God.

There are some wonderful teachers out there. Each soul needs its own way; this is why there are so many teachers. A coat of many colors is still a coat; it fits all together. Sometimes you have to hear the same teaching a few times differently before it will click inside of you. How many times we all have heard someone say, "I have told you that before; how come you didn't listen to me?"

Each person is a learning step for you; with each book and teaching you will know if it is right for you. If it is not, bless and release it, thank it for coming because you might be needing that teaching somewhere down the road. I read and heard things that made no sense to me at the time and came across later when I had assimilated it, and then I understood what it meant.

I have a recommended reading page in the back of some of

my favorite authors. Everything and everybody is a teacher for you, not just the words that you are reading, lessons come from everywhere and meet you where your awareness is. Don't worry about where you are, there is always someone below you on the ladder and someone above you. God meets you at your level and knows exactly what your soul needs.

"The most powerful thing for your biology is forgiveness."

~Carolyn Myss

On the next page is an exercise that came from Reverend Sally Perry, she has graciously allowed me to print it here. This exercise changed my life, but only after I gave up my resistance doing it. Oh my! I was stubborn; I really wanted to hold onto my anger. At one point she said to me, "I am not talking to you anymore until you write forgives and releases, DO NOT call me, until you do." So because she scared the living daylights out of me with that statement, I wrote and wrote and wrote. A lot of pages and when I thought I was done, it allowed some space for more to come up. You have to empty out for more to come in. All the work you do allows for more space for things to come up. If you know it all, how can you be listening and be teachable? All of the steps are teachers for you. You can choose which ones work for you or which ones do not; but if you really want to heal, you have to do this step. There is no way around it.

As Reverend Sally would say, "Do your spiritual homework!"

"Fun stands for finally understanding nothing.
When you have nothing in your mind,
everything you do will be extremely fun."

~ Gary Busey

~Reverend Sally Perry's Forgives and Releases Exercise~

Below is an exercise that is printed with permission from

Reverend Sally Perry's book

Chronicles of a Healer: She Who Dances

"Forgiveness sets my soul free."

~Spirit Medicine

Sleeping under the trees after I had lost my million dollars brought about an ancient connection that I had long ago forgotten. Then the beings of Earth came to teach me about the sun, moon, and the stars, the path of a long ago teaching that had begun to awaken the sensitive part of my nature from childhood and beyond.

In the mornings sounds fell out of my mouth as I tried to still the chatterbox in my brain. Some of the sounds I didn't understand but I felt at peace when I allowed them to flow out. Others were words such as "Jesus," "Peace," "Love," "Joy," and "Patience" that I would chant or sing for ten or fifteen minutes.

Then I felt my mind still, and the Spirit of breath took over to lead my breathing into continuous rhythms. Intervals of holding my breath and then releasing seemed to free my body from tenseness. Slowly I was able to free my mind that had been like a dozen runaway horses all strapped together.

Another process, which I did for four years every day as a part of my meditation, was started when I intended to become a Unity minister. This process I learned later is a part of alcohol and drug rehab groups, also.

I believe this four-year procedure opened the door to the

sub-conscious mind and to cell memory that has allowed me to access some thirty-five past lifetime memories. I had returned to earth to clear up unfinished business, and it always had to do with forgiveness. Forgiveness allowed me to free my soul first and later work with others in this blueprinting process. It works at the DNA level to release cell memory stored in the body from the past.

This simple technique is called forgive and release. I would like to explain the process and show you how to do it. You see I had a lot of anger, hurt and resentment which I had to clear away; or I believe I would have died. My physical, emotional or mental bodies could not have remained intact with all the negative energies that had happened in this life at the time.

Now if you'll get several pieces of paper (I use yellow legal pads), I will start showing you the process beginning with a cleansing that is fifty times more powerful than thoughts and words because it is written.

*Your first list will be titled "**Master List**," and will be numbered one to ten.*

Master List

1.

2.

3.

4.

5.

6.

7.

8.

9.

10.

You will quickly write, without giving much thought, any-one's name who comes to mind whom you need to forgive. Do not analyze, do not block or do not deny anyone's name that comes up. Just write them on your list as quickly as you can. If you didn't add your parents, you are lying to yourself; also your spouse and children must be added.

After you have completed your list of ten people, you have a Master List to start with and on the next sheet of paper you will begin...

Step 1: *Write, "**I forgive and release my mother for....**" Whatever hurts or pains you, you are still carrying today and are projecting towards your mother for causing. Write it down, and don't spare any feelings.*

Step 2: *Write, "**I forgive and release myself for....**" For how you felt about the painful situation. Write it down. It is not complete until you have completed both steps. (REMEMBER: Step 2 is as important as Step 1.)*

*If for some reason, you don't list your mother and your father, you are not being honest with yourself. We all carry resentments from childhood, and the **inner child** needs this healing, even if your parents are deceased. Please, do your spiritual homework.*

The greatest source I know for healing this inner child and the adult self is writing forgives and releases. Every argument or disagreement has to do most likely with the wounded child within us.

Step 3: *Take this sheet of paper that you are writing your for-gives and releases on out of the pad. Tear it up, burn it, bury it, or put it in running water such as a river. You may (for a while) keep it to see exactly how much anger (or resentments and hos-tilities) you held, that you were unaware of. Writing forgives and releases is a sure way to heal. Always remember to purify these thoughts and feelings as I have mentioned above.*

Understanding the energy released when writing something down is very powerful. As we think a thought, we have a chance at that point to cancel that thought and not make it a part of our consciousness. Once we speak it into the world, we have increased its power tenfold. This will take a great deal of extra energy to stop the thought once it is spoken. That is why gossip is so difficult to stop, and is so interchangeable with other people's thoughts and desires-as it creates sickness in the spirit of those gossiped about.

The energy of the written word is fifty times more powerful than your thoughts. Writing impresses the message on the consciousness and the unconsciousness by bridging to imprint in the brain cells and release energy in the emotional intelligence of the body as well.

This process I used for four years every morning faithfully. For myself, I designed an hour meditation. The first fifteen to twenty minutes, and sometimes thirty minutes, writing forgive and releases. Whoever and whatever were weighing heavily on my mind got my attention that morning. This was spiritual house cleaning for my day.

Contact Rev. Sally Perry (Swami Satchidanand) for her book, "Chronicles of a Healer: She who Dances," at East-West Bridge @ 804-749-4679. She offers phone counsel and healings, soul reading and retrieval, medicine wheel, soul growth teachings, sweat lodge, vision quest and ceremonial dances. She honors all people and religions, working for world peace and forgiveness. She can be found on Facebook under EastWestBridge and at Sallybperry@aol.com and www.sallyperry.net, she lives in Rockville, VA.

Copyright Reverend Sally Perry printed with permission from the author and publisher.

~No Fear~

By- Bruce Bailey

I took my fear and held it near

Owned, I let it grow

But in that part deep in my heart

I knew to let it go

On fear I looked and then I took

A step to dissipate it

I saw my soul a thousand fold

Lifetimes would not degrade it.

Not even death with his cold breath

Could harm immortal soul

No cause for doubt, things will work out

That's just the way we roll

And heat of Sun and cold of none

Can't touch me at my core

I lost my fear and shed no tear

I'll be afraid no more!

~Acknowledgements~

To my mother and father:

Chuck and Charlene

Thank you for the lessons of your lives. This book would not be what it is without you. I miss you both.

Some of my teachers along my path:

~Swami Maa/Rev. Sally Perry/Spirit Medicine

Words cannot express how grateful I am for you.

The love I have for you far outpasses my heart level.

Thank you...

~Rina~

Your words of wisdom pulled me through many "amok."

Thank you for believing in me and all the hours you spent with me.

I miss our talks and times together.

~EJ~

My first teacher who started me on the path.

I am forever grateful.

~My friends~

~Paula~

My "partner in crime,"

your support and love. I am at a loss for the words

to say how much this has meant to me. You have been

there for me always, through hell and back.

Thank you & I love you.

~Shelly and Debbie~

For all the lessons about my female side,

I am grateful.

May the rest of your lives be filled with lots of LOVE.

~Claire~

For believing I was "Chanel" when I felt like "Walgreens."

The time I spent with you I will always cherish.

~Fran~

Without our weekly conversations, this book would

have never gotten finished. Thank you so much for

all the encouragement and support.

I love you.

And to all those who have crossed my path and I have not mentioned,

you are thanked and loved.....Including the four- leggeds.

I would be lost without my "Tyger"

and his Mom "Emma."

Emma went to the rainbow bridge on 4-17-2013.

I had not finished the book when we lost her.

She actually helped me heal some unhealed grief

in my heart with her passing. I so love her and

was honored to have her as my dog and our family

dog for thirteen wonderful years of our life.

Her spirit will be extremely missed; she showed me

unconditional love right up until the end of her physical life.

I honor all the animals for their help and support.

We are not even aware of what

all their presence helps us with.

~References~

Rainbow Medicine: Wolf Moon Dance

Life Application Bible

Animal Speaks- Ted Andrews

She Who Dances- Reverend Sally Perry

~Recommended Reading~

Below are some of the books from my own personal collection and only a few to get you started:

The Four Agreements and *The Voice of Knowledge*-Don Miguel Ruiz

The New Earth-Eckhart Tolle

Chronicles of a Healer-Reverend Sally Perry

You Can Heal Your Life-Louise Hay

Fearless Living-Rhonda Britten

Animal Speaks-Ted Andrews

In Your Dreams-Mary Summer Rain

Spiritual Unfoldment Books 1-4-White Eagle

Jumping Mouse-Mary Elizabeth Marlow

Magnificence-Maureen Sullivan

Power vs Force-David R. Hawkins

Right Use Of Will-Ceanne DeRohan

A Search for God Book 1 & 2-Edgar Cayce

The Light Shall Set You Free-Norma J. Milanovich and Shirley D. McCune

One Day My Soul Just Opened Up-Iyanla Vanzant

The Twelve Powers of Man-Charles Fillmore

Invisible Acts of Power-Carolyn Myss

Feelings Buried Alive Never Die-Karol Truman

Your Body Speaks Your Mind-Deb Shaprio

The Shack-Wm. Paul Young

Love Is Letting Go of Fear-Gerald G. Jampolsky

Your Body's Telling You: Love Yourself –Lise Bourbeau

~Notes~

Cintra Best

Enlighten My Senses

~About the author~

Cintra Best is a spiritual seeker, business owner and creator of "Enlighten My Senses." Her extensive background in self-help, along with her Bachelor's and Doctorate in Natural Health, helps her in coaching and writing worldwide. She writes a column called "Holistic Corner" which is on her blog. She is currently writing her second book-*"Enlighten Your World."* She enjoys living with her family and her dog at their Wild Turkey Inn in Nebraska and in her spare time she has created her own line of Green Chili Sauce.

~About the book~

Enlighten My Senses is a story about the journey that one woman took to open her heart and her life. It walks you, the reader, down a path that shows how your history, heritage and emotions affect your well-being. It guides you to look inside and outside step-by-step to help and support yourself in bringing light to areas that you may not have been aware of. Get ready for a whole new way to look at and improve your world!

CPSIA information can be obtained
at www.ICGtesting.com
Printed in the USA
LVOW10s0320110917
548250LV00022B/1667/P